LEAVING OKLAHOMA

LC Rung

Copyright © 2020. LC Rung

All rights reserved.

ISBN-13: 978-1-7328440-1-8 (paperback),
978-1-7328440-2-5 (ebook)

Library of Congress Control Number: 2020918269

First edition September 2020, Montville: Leah Szalai. Printed in the United States of America.

No part of this book may be reproduced, distributed, or transmitted in any form or by any means, without written permission from the publisher, except for brief quotations in critical reviews and other noncommercial uses as permitted by copyright law. For permission requests, send an email to lcrung@outlook.com.

This book is a work of fiction. Names, characters, businesses, places, and events are either products of the author's imagination or are used fictitiously. Any resemblance to actual people (living or dead) is purely coincidental.

to my family

LEAVING OKLAHOMA

RUSH

CHAPTER 1

Lumpy Dies

The air gets a little thin up there at ten thousand feet. See, oxygen is hard to come by in the mountains. Something about them little particles just not wanting to be next to each other anymore. Your brain swells as it suffocates, pushing out, what I have to assume, is any ability to be a rational, normal person. That's the only explanation I have for that godforsaken town and the people in it. Lord knows I ain't no saint, but I ain't ever done nothing like the people in that town done to me.

I moved there willingly. I know I did. I put a few cardboard boxes in the back of that old, red truck and kissed my mama goodbye. That was the last time I ever saw her or that tiny house in Oklahoma. My mama told me she wasn't going to say goodbye, because I was "a stubborn fool, hell-bent on breaking her heart," but that woman never could be mad at me for more than a minute. Just as I put my boot on that rusty truck step, she came running out of the house and wrapped her arms around me. They were strong, built up from years of farming that land, and she let me feel just how disappointed she was.

She looked up at me and said, "Rush, now why do you want to go and leave Fairhope and your poor mama?"

I don't think I'll ever forget that moment. I remember exactly what I said, but only because it was about the dumbest thing I could say. She probably thought so too, right until the day she died, but she was too nice to ever say so.

"There ain't nothing more important than seeing new places," I told her.

"Even me?" she asked, her eyes the saddest I ever seen them.

"Even you, Mama."

That's what I told her, anyways. I guess the real reason I left was because I was running away. I never admitted that to nobody but my best friend, Ricky. He was the one who told me about Silverheel, a tiny town on top of the highest mountain in Montana. Ricky said it was the best kind of place for hiding from the rest of the world, and he was right. You could disappear—whether you were meaning to or not.

I s'ppose that I should back up. It was June 14, 2002—halfway through my nineteenth year

—when I left my mama in Fairhope and headed northwest. I drove past the glowing wind turbines in Kansas, through the endless rows of Nebraskan corn, into the desolate lands of South Dakota, and up those narrow, winding mountain roads. I got to Silverheel, Montana, twenty-one hours later.

It was summer then, so only the very tips of the mountains had a cap of snow. The rest were a blend of dark green pines and red rock. The wild goats and sheep would stand on the cliffs and look out at the cars as they drove by beneath, like self-appointed watchdogs of the mountains.

Come winter, the entire mountain would be buried under pure snow that glittered in the sun. The lakes would be frozen white too, but you could sometimes spot a bright red tent that someone pitched to ice fish in.

Silverheel was nice in the beginning. The first time I drove into town was the first time I felt like I could breathe. I stepped out of that truck and just stood there, in the middle of Main Street, for a good five minutes, taking in the giant mountains that surrounded me. The funny thing about mountains is that they remind you how small you are—it ain't nothing like living on flat ground, where it's easy to forget that you ain't nobody or no-thing.

Main Street was lined with buildings from the 1800s. It looked like a scene out of the Wild West movies that I'd watch with my pa. There was a hotel-turned-homeless-shelter on the corner—a three-story, brick building with rows and rows of windows. And there were plenty of the old-style saloons with worn, wood siding and upper decks. Silverheel didn't have much in the way of businesses—a coffee shop, a grocery store, a couple bars and dispens'ries—but all of them were on Main Street.

The people there, they seemed like good people at first. We were sick of the gov'ment and their rules. Sick of this modern way of life. Silverheel was our escape. But I s'ppose that's my inner-hippie talking. Gen, my girlfriend, always told me that I had an inner- and an outer-hippie. The inner-hippie was the one that wanted to hide away and live off the land. The outer-hippie was the one that hung blacklight posters on them walls and kept stickers from my fav'rite dispens'ry. Gen never did like either of those hippies.

But that was probably because Gen thought something of herself. She had four names—Imogen Delilah Mae Tucker—and I always s'pected that she placed a lot of emphasis on that extra name, like it added a sort of fanciness that us three-namers don't have.

I lived in Silverheel first. Gen followed a few years later in '04. She was never really cut out for a place like that. Not at first, at least. We should have known that when we were talking about her moving out there. Too in love to even think about it, I guess. But Silverheel ain't like the rest of the world. It's hidden deep in the mountains, where laws ain't nothing more than the ink they're written in.

I never did go to no fancy college, but I wasn't stupid. I knew that I had to look out for myself in a town like Silverheel. I wasn't the least bit scared, though. I had my grandaddy's gun—a fine revolver with a wood grain handle and blued steel barrel—and the plumb dumb confidence that comes with being nineteen.

About seven years after I moved to Silverheel, a filthy vermin by the name of Art McCraw tried to trick me out of twel—, well, it was more than a thousand dollars, anyways. He came by, door-to-door, selling something or the other. Now, I always was the kind of guy to talk to someone who knocks on my door. Gen, though, she hated it. She'd give me a hard time for talking to door-knockers. Said it was just encouraging them to come back. If it was up to her, she'd hide in the other room while they stood on the porch, knocking and knocking, until they got the hint and left.

But I didn't mind hearing what people have to say because I liked making them happy—and it almost paid off that day, too. Art and I got to talking about some land further down the mountain. He told me that he got a pot farm down there and that he was looking for a business partner. Well, I was always looking for a way to make some money so that I could take care of me and Gen. And I knew from watching the TV that you got to invest your money like them men on Wall Street do, so

I thought to myself, I thought, *Rush, this is a good deal.* Well, it turns out that his pot farm ain't nothing more than a few wilted plants in a run-down cabin, but the sheriff didn't do a darn thing about it. All he said was that he was going to look into it. So, one night, I was sitting in my living room, having a few beers and stewing. I was sitting and stewing, and I got a mind to set Art straight on my own. I headed to Main Street and waited real quiet-like behind a building because I knew that he walked home from the liquor store everyday around seven o'clock.

It was cold out—must have been negative ten degrees—but I waited until I saw him come around the corner, and then I jumped out from behind that building. He was a big boy, Nebraskan-grown, but I shoved him to the ground and made a pretty, little circle on his cheek with the end of my grandaddy's revolver. I told Art that I better not see him around Silverheel no more.

That same year, Kenny Jones got a bug up his butt and thought himself smart to cut my brake lines. He was mad at me because I told his pa that he was beating on his granmom, but that woman was a screaming and a hollering, and there ain't no way I could have just let him go on beating on her like that. So that son-of-a-gun Kenny was fixing to take me out by making little cuts in my brakes.

He almost did it, too. My brakes blew out as I was driving to work the next morning. I must have been going about a hundred miles an hour down that mountain. Luckily, those roads have plenty of them runaway truck ramps for semis. I would have been dead in the ground if not for them ramps.

I knew right away that it was that low-life, Kenny. I didn't even bother with no sheriff that time. I tracked him all the way to Whitefish and greeted him the same kind of way as I did Art. I heard he left town a few days after that.

I found plenty of trouble in the ten years that I lived in Silverheel, but I always held my own —until the winter of 2013, that is. I took care of those jerks, Kenny and Art, but there was one person who outsmarted me. You can't trust anyone, even the people you think you know. Not in Silverheel. That was when I realized something about the gov'ment. They're dangerous in their own right, but they can offer you protections. Protections I never knew I needed until I didn't have them no more.

My memory's never been too good, but I know that it was February 13, 2013, when it all started. I know for a fact that was the date because all the numbers added up to twel—. Well, the fact is that it was twelve. They added up to twelve. Here's the math, plain and simple:

February is the second month, so that's 2.
It was the 13th, so that's 1 + 3
And the year was 2013, so 2 + 0 + 1 + 3

Altogether, that's twelve. No two ways around

it.

Gen used to roll her big, hazel eyes whenever I'd bring it up, but I always knew twelve was no good for me. Everything bad that's ever happened to me, happened because of twelve. I know this for a fact.

1. I was twelve when my pa walked out on us.
2. It was December when the bank took the farm from my mama.
3. I had twelve candy bars in my box when I knocked on Victor's door.
4. There were twelve cars in the parking lot the night I did the bad thing.

I knew twelve was no good, so I did my very best to stay far, far away from it—I wouldn't even let poor Gen buy a dozen donuts. I told her there was no way in heck she was bringing that box in my truck and that she better get to eating. She grumbled and stomped her feet, but I'll be damned if she didn't stand in that snowy, grocery store parking lot, shoving a powdered jelly donut in her mouth.

But High Alps Ski Resort don't care if the numbers add up to twelve, so Gen and I had to work on February 13, 2013. There ain't no jobs in Silverheel, so we were lucky to find pay at High Alps, just twenty minutes down the pass. She worked in the lodge, serving coffees and hot chocolates in that cute, little apron, and I was a lift attendant, making sure them chairlifts were loading right. I was real proud when I got that job, because I ain't ever been an attendant before.

Those were our winter jobs. We had to find different work come summer. Summer in the mountains is short, about three months long from June to August, but, boy, was it the best time to be in Silverheel. Gen and I would hike to Panguitch Lake when it was real hot out. We didn't always have enough money for food, so we'd fish if we were hungry. Other days, though, we'd just lie by the cool, blue water until we were cooking under that hot sun and just dying to jump in the lake.

I'd watch Gen walk real slow to the edge of the water. She'd stand there for a moment and peek back at me before starting to unbutton her shorts. We didn't have no bathing suits, so she'd act real shy, like good Southern girls are s'pposed to do, but it was all for show. She knew she was the most beautiful girl to ever grace God's earth. And me? I certainly didn't waste no time following her into the water. We'd float together until the sun disappeared over the mountains.

When we felt like dealing with Wilbur James, we'd head down to work at Wilbur's White-Water Retreat. He'd always twist his face up when he saw us because he was mad that we didn't show up for work every day. But he didn't have much choice. No one else was willing to put up with him. Gen and I learned to just ignore him whenever he'd march over, high as a kite, and start accusing us of something or another.

Gen sold ice cream cones, and I guided the rafts. Tourists would come up from those fancy states, like California or Washin'ton, and pay Wilbur a whole one-hundred-dollar bill to go for a ride on the river, like they thought it was some darn amusement park or something. I don't think they realized they could die, that the water could swallow them up, just like that. They just signed their name on that waiver without a care in the world, like they were signing up for cable.

I almost went to see the good Lord when we were training to be river guides. Everything was going along fine until we hit a rough patch of water and then *bam*! My raft tipped, and just like that, I was plunged into the icy water. That's how it always happens too: it's fine until it's not. I tried to get my body right (head upstream, feet downstream) but my foot was stuck between the rocks on the bottom of the river. The frothy, white current was rushing against my back, and it kept my face in the water, just the same as I used to do to my brother, Eli, at the public pool.

There was nothing I could do but think about Gen and how much I loved her. I remember exactly how that felt, too. My lungs were burning but the thought of never seeing Gen again hurt even more. I didn't end up losing Gen, though. Not that day, at least. One of the other guides pulled me onto the big, jagged rocks that lined the bank. I was thanking the good Lord that Wilbur had enough sense to teach us CPR on the first day of river-guide class.

Gen called that my near-death experience. She said that she always wanted one of them, just to see what it's like to die. She thought it would make her less afraid of death, or some nonsense like that. Well, I can tell you that I'm as good as dead right now, and it ain't nothing like what I went through that day on the river. It's a heck of a lot worse.

But most summer days, we didn't have much going on. I'd watch her walk around in those cutoff shorts all day until, finally, eight o'clock would come around and her soft skin would be next to mine. We'd sleep by the river each night, on account of how far it was to get to town.

"Dirty vagabonds," Wilbur would sneer at us, because we'd just move our tent to wherever we felt like sleeping that night. Gen would say she was feeling lucky so we'd go look for old coins up near the abandoned mining district, or I'd say that we should hike down Longneck Trail, and we'd just pack up and go. We didn't stay in any one place for long, but we were always together.

Each night would start the same: I'd take out our coffee-can stove and fry us some perch before passing her a joint. She'd whisper to me in the dark, pausing whenever she'd hear the cy'otes yipping in the background.

"What do you think they're saying?" Gen would ask, twirling the ends of her auburn hair that had begun to gather in accidental dreadlocks.

I looked at that girl, her mind full of wonder. She was always wanting to know the answers to things. Always learning and reading. She'd pick up a phone book if there was nothing else to read. She was real smart like that. I didn't always have the answers, but I gave her my best.

"He sounds sad, like his friend died."

I picked at some bark on a log. I was satisfied with my answer, but she must not have been, because she came right back with another question:

"Where do you think we go when we die?"

That one was harder. My mama wanted me to believe in Heaven, and I did for a long time, until I started realizing there was no way God was going to let me in. And I sure didn't want to believe I was destined for the *other* place, so I started hoping for something else—hoping that we get a second chance.

"I think we don't move on until our souls are at peace," I told Gen.

"Why are you here then?" She didn't miss a beat.

I walked right into that one, I s'ppose. There was so much I wanted to tell her, but I knew I couldn't. She'd be gone before the sun came up if I told her the full truth. So, I told her part of it.

"Fear. I feel like I've been running for a long time. You help me forget, though."

She wrapped her fingers around mine and moved her lips real close to my ear. "I love you," she whispered.

I paused, real long. Too long, probably, because I could see her tiny nose start to wrinkle in the moonlight. But I wasn't trying to fig're out if I loved her. I already knew I did. I was just upset she said it first.

I said, "Gen, I do love you, but the boy's s'pposed to say it first. That's all."

But that girl always was too impatient. She never could wait for nothing or no one. That was just one of the things I loved about her.

We never did have no problems in the summer; it was always the winter. I think the snow made her mad. It brought out her crazy. She hated the snow, but she loved them Oklahoma tornados. We'd sit and watch the sky go black when we were younger. A biggin was rolling in on the day we met. We were only thirteen when I saw her at that dairy stand in the middle of Fairhope. She was up on her tiptoes in cheap flip-flops that were falling apart at the seams, telling the ice cream lady that she wasn't swirling the custard on her cone right.

"Miss, your swirls ain't even. See that side right there? It's dipping down over the edge," I heard Gen say to the lady, not even trying to hide the impatience in her voice.

Gen tried to explain a few more times before just plain giving up and barging behind the counter. She snatched that cone from the lady's hand and threw it right in the trash.

"This is how you do it," Gen said as she grabbed a fresh cone and pulled the lever. "It'll come real fast now, so you got to be ready. You got to move the cone towards the spout, gentle circles, just like this. You got to keep your hand straight, like this—see? That's why your swirls were tipping over the edge."

That poor lady's face was red with anger, but I couldn't help but smile. Gen switched the lever off and held up the most perfectly-swirled cone that I ever did see, balanced right in the middle with no edges falling down the side. I asked Gen how long she been swirling ice cream, and she said that it was her first time. She was good at things without even trying, which was good for her because she was a perfectionist, and she wasn't going to settle for anything less. It was also good for everyone around her, because when Gen didn't get what she wanted, we were all in for it.

I should have known she was trouble then. Instead, I just walked right up to her and put fifty cents down on the counter. Because I knew right then that I wanted to buy her ice creams for the rest of my life. We took our cones back to my house and watched the tornado move in from my front porch. She'd take her eyes off the dark sky just long enough to lick the sticky custard that was melting onto her fingers. I'd take my eyes off of her just long enough to glance at the sky.

That was a good day—probably because the numbers didn't add up to twelve, if I had to guess. But on February 13, 2013, they did. There's no getting around the math. It was winter, so you know

Gen was already a little crazy from the snow, and work that day just about set her over the edge.

Gen told me she was taking orders when these two guys walked into the lodge and had a seat on the purple velvet sofa. *Crushed. Crushed velvet, Rush*, she'd probably say right now if she could hear me, because details always did matter to her. But I ain't able to tell the difference. Velvet is velvet, anyways.

So, these guys come in. They take off their ski goggles and unzip their brightly-colored, puffy jackets.

Those jackets are real warm. Should be, for how 'spensive they are. You could feed a whole family for a month for what those jackets cost. They sold them in the shops around High Alps—I seen one for four hundred dollars one time. Four hundred. I don't think all the jackets I ever had in my life cost that much.

But High Alps is in a resort town, so just about everyone who goes there has the kind of money to buy four-hundred-dollar jackets that you only wear on vacation. Some of them are doctors, a lot of them are lawyers—all those jobs that give you the kind of money that makes you ski in the winter and golf in the summer. I guess I should feel real lucky that I never had that kind of money because golf is just about the most boring sport I could think of.

"Hey hon, how about a triple foam, soy latte?" One of the men snapped his fingers at Gen.

Gen liked to name people. I think she had a certain amount of meanness in her that had nowhere to go most days, so she found a way to use it by giving people nicknames. Now, she'd never say them to anyone's face, of course. It took me three whole years to find out what mine was.

"Come on, tell me," I begged her one day as she was doing the dishes.

"Nope."

"I'll finish the dishes if you tell me."

She made me beg her a few more times before she finally gave in. I think she liked the chase.

"Fine." She dropped the sponge in the sink and turned to look at me. "Sometimes, I call you Blame-shifter Bill."

"What? Why?"

"Because you're always putting the blame on someone else."

"No, I don't," I fired back.

"Oh, yes. You absolutely do! It's always everyone's fault but your own."

I wasn't much in the mood to do the dishes after that, which *really was* Gen's fault if you stop and think about it.

The guys in the lodge didn't have it any better: Hemorrhoids, for the one who ordered the latte, because he leaned to one side when he sat, like he was fav'rin a cheek. And Gen named his friend Mr. Construction, on account of the amount of gel in his hair looking like he could walk on any construction site and not need a hard hat.

"We don't have no soy." Gen did her best to look sorry that she didn't have no vegetable milk for the men.

"My God, we might as well be in the Midwest with the rest of the melonheads." Mr. Construction rolled his eyes.

"What'd you say?" Gen put her hand on her hip. The men didn't know her well enough, but that was the first warning sign. You have to be real observant when you're dealing with Gen. She'll give you signs she's unhappy, like how a dog'll lift his lip, but you only get a couple, and if you don't see them, well then, that's on you.

"What's the matter, darling? Can't hear anything over that accent of yours?"

That was strike two for the men.

Now, I don't know exactly what happened after that, because Gen's story was a little different from everyone else's. But I do know that I heard Gen yelling from clear across the hill, and boy, was I glad to not be on the receiving end of it that time. The manager sent Gen to bake scones after that. He told her she couldn't talk to the customers no more.

Gen stayed in the back, rolling dough all the way up to five o'clock, when we were allowed to leave for the day. We started hitchhiking home because my truck died a few months back, and we didn't have no money to fix it. So, we set up the mountain, like we did every day, sticking out our thumbs whenever we'd see someone drive by.

We'd usually luck out before too long and see ole Lumpy come driving down the road in his beater.

Lumpy had his own taxi business, so he was always driving around. He could have made some good money doing that, on account of most people in Silverheel not affording a car. But he was just about the worst businessman you ever did meet. You'd call him for a ride and he'd forget to show up, or you'd be driving and he'd forget where he was taking you. Probably smoked too much pot. But he was always dressed in the finest clothes—I never saw him in anything but a black suit. And he was nice, real nice. He'd pick me and Gen up for free and take us anywhere we'd want to go. Probably another reason he never did make no money with that taxi.

So, on February 13, 2013, Gen and I are hitching, and it's a whiteout, but just in the distance, I see Terry Higgins stumbling down the side of the road. Now, Terry never had been sober a day in his life. Not for as long as I knew him, anyway. Lola Jean, from down at the coffee shop, told me about how Terry's boy was lost in an avalanche. They were doing some winter camping up in the mountains, and Terry triggered a snow slide, just from walking around up there.

Being buried in an avalanche is the slow kind of death you'd only wish on your enemy. The snow starts moving under your feet, and it takes you with it. More snow comes from further up the mountain until you're three feet under.

You can breathe under the snow, but it's a lot like when you got your head under the blankets for too long. Each breath gets a little less satisfying than the last. The snow's too heavy to move, so you sit and wait. You wait for someone to find you, or you wait to die. Eleven minutes. That's all it takes. They found Terry's boy at minute fifteen. Terry was never quite right after that.

Terry rubbed most people the wrong way. They didn't understand him, didn't take the time to know his pain. Not Lumpy, though. Lumpy was always looking out for Terry. One day, Lola Jean was walking home from the grocery store, and she saw Terry sitting on a bench in the middle of a blizzard. He was half-froze when she found him. She tried to get him up, but he was using his last bit of energy to fight her off. He wouldn't get up for nothing. So, she called Lumpy to come help, and Lumpy knew just how to talk to him. He got Terry up off that bench and drove him home. That was the kind of guy Lumpy was.

"Look at that fool, Terry." I nudged Gen as we walked home. "He's as gone as the sun."

"Here comes Lumpy," Gen grumbled, ignoring me. She was relieved to be done with the weather and the hitching.

We could hear Lumpy's car before we could see him on account of the whiteout. But I heard his four-cylinder struggling to climb the hill. And just as Lumpy comes up over the hill, Terry decides he don't want to be on that side of the road no more.

So, he darts straight in front of Lumpy. Straight in front of him, like one of those deer on the highway. Lumpy swerved to avoid hitting him, but he cut his wheel too hard on the icy road and sent his car off the cliff.

Gen screamed and took off after the car, worried sick about Lumpy. Things might have turned out differently for Lumpy if Silverheel salted their roads instead of putting sand down, but there was nothing left of the car by the time it landed at the bottom of the cliff. All the sides were smashed in from bouncing off rocks on the way down—there was a reason they had a celebration of life instead of a wake. Gen just fell in the snow and sobbed and sobbed for poor Lumpy.

We called in sick for the next day because Gen was in no shape to be serving coffee after that. We sat on our green, hand-me-down couch in the corner of our small living room. She was quiet for a real long time, and I started to worry about her. I ain't ever known her to be quiet for so long. That girl could talk and talk about any little thing you could think of. She had enough opinions to fill a book, maybe two.

One time, our high school teacher gave us a quiz that had some question about punishing one of the students. Something about whether a student should be allowed to go to the school dance that Friday after breaking one of the rules. Gen's hand shot straight up the moment that paper hit her desk—you'd think she was on a game show set to win a million dollars or something. She let Ms. Booker know, right there in the middle of class, just how inappropriate she thought that question was.

One of the first experiments that we did in that class was drop a mint into soda. You had to get your hand out of the way real fast, because the soda would bubble and shoot straight out of the bottle. That's how I liked to describe Gen: she was like a bottle of soda, just waiting for a mint to be dropped in. She had way too much backbone than should've been able to fit inside her five-foot-two body.

She was nothing like that after Lumpy died, though. I didn't recognize her no more.

"You okay, Gen?" I put my arm around her thin shoulder.

"I want to go home," she cried.

"We are home." I was really worrying about that girl's brain at that point. I thought the snow might've finally done her in.

"Home," she repeated. "Oklahoma."

I paused, for a long time again. But it wasn't because I was upset she gone and said it first. It was because I knew she wasn't going to like what I had to say. I said, "I ain't moving back to Oklahoma, Gen."

She scrunched her face up in anger. "I left everything behind when I moved here for you. You promised that if I didn't like it, we could move back."

"Oklahoma just ain't where I belong." I looked at her over the edge of my cup as I took a sip of cold, weak coffee, hoping that she'd accept my reasoning. I fed her the same line I always did whenever she'd bring it up. *Oklahoma ain't where I belong.* I never gave her no more than that. It was just enough of a story for her to accept, but not enough for her to ever feel like she really did understand.

It was a lot like when those smooth-talking, New York politicians say that they're the best thing for this country on account of them being able to make the country better. You nod your head, thinking that they made sense, but when you walk away, you realize that they didn't really say anything in the first place. Those are the kind of answers I'd give Gen. Non-answers, really.

"Lumpy's gone, Rush. That could be any one of us. I don't want to be away from my family no more," Gen argued as tears fell down her cheeks and onto her jeans.

I rubbed Gen's back and gave her my best at comforting, but I was never too good at that women stuff. I wanted to give Gen what she wanted. I wanted to give her the whole world. I didn't have a choice though. Going back to Oklahoma just wasn't an option.

"I'm sorry, Gen. I am. But I won't go," I told her.

Can't go was closer to the truth, but I fig'red that would be opening myself up to too many questions.

"I'll go without you then!" Gen stood up in a fresh rush of anger. "That was always the back-up plan. Do you remember? Do you remember me saying that to you before I even moved out here? Because deep down, I knew you'd go and do this to me. I knew it."

Gen always had back-up plans. Her mama taught her to always be thinking two, three steps ahead. But there was one thing she didn't plan for.

"Ain't you forgetting something?" I nodded toward our seven-month-old, Penny, who was happily parked in front of the TV.

She was twenty-nine weeks that day, I can hear Gen's voice now, buzzing around my head like a pesky housefly.

Our fighting had been enough to drown out the British cartoon show that Penny was watching, but we were now painstakin'ly aware of it. It was Penny's favorite show, a fast-acting antidote for fussiness that we applied liberally and as often as necessary, but sometimes, I had half a mind to claw my ear drums out.

This show is Britain's way of getting back at us for the American revolution, I thought, impressing myself with my cleverness. I wanted so badly to say it to Gen, but we were in the middle of a fight, so I said this instead:

"If you're leaving, you ain't taking Penny. Is that what you want, Gen? You want Penny to grow up without no mama?"

I think that's what they call irony—when the

opposite of what you're saying is what ends up happening, or something like that. In which case, it doesn't get more ironic than that, because Penny wasn't about to lose her mama. She was about to lose her pa. I just didn't know it yet.

I didn't have no warning, no flashing neons or nothing like that. I had no idea that I was about to become one of The Missing. But here I am, missing for more than seven years. At least, I think that's how long it's been. The days go on and on sometimes—like a string of black nothingness. No sounds, no smells, no tastes, nothing that I can touch.

Seven years, one hundred and forty-two days, Gen's voice corrects me.

My only hope is that somebody finds me someday—or finds my body, if you want to be technical.

I spend a lot of time thinking about the days leading up to my disappearance. I guess that's why I want to tell my story now—maybe if I can get it out then it won't be stuck in my head no more. I won't have to ask myself the same questions, over and over again: Was there something I could have done? Something that would have saved me? And then there's the question that scares me the most: Did I ever do anything at all? Because if I really think about it, I s'ppose the truth is that I never did do anything. I lived my life without ever having any real goals or dreams, so I guess I shouldn't be too surprised that someone found it so easy to take.

It was the wildest thing, though. Disappearing made me instantly famous. Or, infamous, maybe, depending on which story you believed. And I didn't do a thing to earn that fame. It was all because of something that was done *to* me.

I have to admit that Eli chose a darn good picture for my missing posters. It was a photo that he took the day I left Oklahoma, when I was nineteen and he was seventeen. I remember standing in front of my truck, thinking that I was going to spend the rest of my life out west. Turns out, the rest of my life was only ten more years.

The news people put that photo on every station for the first few weeks. The camera guy would zoom in on my face as the ladies took guesses about what could have happened to me. Not a single one of them got it right, though. I guess I can't really blame them. I would have called you a darn fool if you had told me what was about to happen to me.

Eli was on the news a few times with Gen, telling them about what kind of person I was.

"Trusting to a fault," he said, shooting an undeniable glare at Gen.

And, believe it or not, Gen even managed to look a little sad.

CHAPTER 2

Trapped Animals

There are only two things that I consider mysteries in life. The rest of the world is solvable, through physics and stuff like that; it's predictable. You do something, you get an equal something back, or however that saying goes. But there are two things that just don't have no explanation.

One: when I was eighteen and still living at my mama's house, I snuck out of my room, past my mama watching soaps in the living room, to hide something in the hole behind the shed. I'm not going to say what it was, because it's not the polite kind of thing to talk about, but it was the kind of thing you don't want your mama to find. So, I dug a few inches down, taking extra measures to make sure it was buried in there real good. Three days later, I go to get a gas can out of the shed, and there it was, just lying on the ground, a foot away from the hole. To this day, I have no idea how it got there.

Two: there was an ice cream carton glued to the floor in the house that me and Gen rented. It was there when we moved in. Gen and I racked our brains, trying to fig're out why someone would even do that, but we never could understand it.

I'd take a knife and hack at the empty container whenever I needed to get away from Gen for a while because we were fighting. We were fighting a lot lately, so I got almost half of it up in just one week.

The hacking was meant to take my mind off things, but it really only made me think about Gen more. We were eating peanut butter ice cream that day I met her at the dairy stand. I ain't ever had peanut butter ice cream before that. I wanted chocolate, but Gen wouldn't let me.

"See, ain't this better than plain ole chocolate?" she asked as we sat on my porch, waiting for the storm.

It wasn't. I missed the familiarity of chocolate. The safety of it. But I was more concerned about how dark that sky was getting than missing out on a chocolate cone.

"Don't you want to go inside now, Gen?" I eyed the funnel in the distance.

"Don't be a baby. It's just getting good," she said.

The dust kicked up around the house, and I looked back at the door. It was shaking violently against the frame. No matter how much I wanted to convince myself that I was a man at thirteen, I wanted nothing more than to go hide with my mama down in the cellar.

"I'm going inside," I said as I stood in the doorway, waiting for Gen to reply, but she peeled the wrapper off her cone and pretended like she didn't hear me. I later learned that this was something she did quite a lot.

By the time the storm passed over, and I came back outside, she was gone. I saw her in school after that, but I never did say nothing to her. I just fig'red I blew it. We graduated in 2001, and I didn't see Gen again until a couple years after I moved to Montana.

We had just gotten some weather, about three feet of snow, and I was outside shoveling a path on the sidewalk. The last person I ever expected to see was Gen, but there she was, strolling down the path I had just made, headed straight towards me.

"Gen?" I called out.

"Can I help you?" She stopped and took a couple steps backward, like she thought I had plans to hurt her. (Me, hurt her—ha!)

"It's me, Rush."

She studied my face, but I could tell she didn't remember me. I guess I looked a little bit different from the last time we saw each other. I had the same dark brown hair, but it was almost down to my ears by then, and I didn't have no beard when we were younger.

"I, uh, I bought your ice cream when we were thirteen, remember? You were yelling at the dairy lady and then we sat on my porch and watched the tornado roll in."

"You know, Rush, I remember that day a little differently. I remember *helping* the dairy lady learn how to swirl a proper cone. And then I remember sitting on your front porch, *by myself*." She lowered her eyebrows, making sure I was about to remember it the same way.

"You're right," I laughed. "I went down to the cellar and left you on my porch. I am sorry about that, by the way."

"You still a runner, Rush Kilmer?"

Yes.

"No."

"What are you doing all the way out here, then?" She folded her arms across her chest, like she had caught me in my first lie to her (which, in fact, she had). I told you—she never missed a beat.

Luckily for me, though, I had been asked that question enough times that I already had an answer prepared, and it came out smooth, just as smooth as the truth would have.

"I just like the mountains. Why are you doing out here, anyhow?"

"I'm the lead in a play at the opera house tomorrow night." She smiled, proud to call herself a touring actor.

"Any chance you want to come inside?"

"You're always wanting to go inside."

I hung my head in agreement before peeking back up at her. "Well, I'm hoping you're going to come with me this time."

And she did. We only had the weekend together, but that same feeling I had when we were thirteen came right back. I knew she was the one I was meant to be with. Ricky would give me crap if he heard me talking like this, but I really felt like I had found my soulmate.

Gen called it a wild kind of love. She said she knew right away that she would follow me to the ends of the earth. And, somehow, I knew right away that I would take her there.

I put on a button-down and my best jeans and went to the opera house every night that weekend. That was the first, and only, play I ever saw, so I don't got nothing to compare it to, but it sure suited me well. And, boy, did I love watching Gen up there. She stole the whole show, in my opinion.

Come Monday morning, we were standing on Main Street in front of the bus that was s'pposed to take her back to Oklahoma. It was so hard saying goodbye to that girl. It was winter, so it must have been plenty cold out, but all I remember is feeling like my whole body was on fire. Every inch of me wanted to grab her and keep her from leaving. I was hoping that she felt the same way about me as I did her.

"Will you drop me a dime?" I asked her.

Gen tilted her head. "A dime?"

"You know, say hi."

"Rush." She rolled her eyes. "That means you're going to tattle on someone."

"No, it doesn't." I shook my head adamantly. "It means that you're going to put a dime in the payphone to give someone a call."

"Yeah—the *police*."

"Well, I'll be dropping you a dime," I whispered to her but she was already stepping onto the bus.

And I did drop her a dime. I called her almost as soon as her bus got back to Oklahoma, and we spent the next couple of months talking on the phone every day. We'd talk for hours and hours.

"What happens if I get homesick?" she asked me after we started talking about her moving to Silverheel.

"If you absolutely hate it after a couple years, we'll go back. I really hate Oklahoma, Gen, but I love you, and now that I found you, I'm not letting you go."

I don't really know why I said that. Part of me knew that I could never go back. I guess I was just hoping that she'd move out there and not want to leave. But Gen took what I said to heart and started looking for a place in Silverheel right away.

I had been couch-surfing ever since I got to Montana, and if it taught me anything, it taught me that there were a lot of bad houses in Silverheel. I wanted to find a house that was just right, with good ins'lation. But that was hard to come by, and Gen was impatient. She made us choose the first house that we could find.

We ended up in a house that was built in the 1800s, like most were in Silverheel. The houses used to sit up above the tree line, by the old mining camps. When the iron dried up, they plopped the houses down in the center of town—right on top of each other, gutter to gutter. The outsides had fancy wood molding, painted in bright yellows and blues, but the insides were bone-chilling cold.

"Can we please turn the heat up?" Gen's teeth chattered as she sat under a scratchy, wool blanket.

"It won't do no good, Gen," I told her for the hundredth time.

In my mind, I scolded her for being so impatient. I was just itching to say those four golden words: *I told you so*. But I thought better of it.

Instead, I tried telling her that the house doesn't hold no heat. She didn't want to hear it though—she insisted the house was cold because it was haunted by three and a half ghosts. The haunting, of course, was not something she could've known ahead of time, so it was not her fault for choosing a bad house, she reasoned.

I asked Gen, "How can there be three and a half ghosts?"

She never really did explain that one. She just told me some story about a milkmaid who let a barrel of milk sit out in the warm sun for a few days in 1848. The milkmaid didn't want to get sent to the whipping stocks for spoiling precious milk, so she didn't tell nobody about it. But the little bugs had already started growing in there from it being in the sun for so long.

They weren't the good kind of bugs either, like the mudbugs that you catch for dinner down in the Oklahoma rivers. They were the bad bugs, the invisible kind that make your stomach hurt. My pa got rabbit fever once; the doctor said it was from some roadkill that Mama cooked up. I can still hear him screaming as he clutched his stomach and rolled back and forth in the bed. Well, I'd imagine that those little milk bugs made the whole town look just like Pa did.

Gen said dysentery'll run you dry until you ain't got no water left in you. That's how it killed so many people in Silverheel in 1848, including the family that used to live where Gen and I lived. She said that's why it was so cold in there. But Gen was wrong about the ghosts. The houses were over two hundred years old, so the heat just went right out of them. It never did get above fifty degrees in there because we couldn't afford to be pumping heat for no reason.

Each night, we'd light the stove, and I'd shove a towel under the door to try to keep what little heat in that we could. And then Gen would follow behind me and adjust the towel because I never could do nothing to her specifications.

We'd put on our underwear, then our long underwear, then our long pajamas and a pair of thick socks, but no amount of flannel could have warmed up the cold between me and Gen that night Lumpy died.

She was scooted all the way to the edge of the mattress, about as far away as she could get from me. She was so close to the edge that the weight of her body was sinking it to the floor. I don't blame her, I guess. I'd be far away from me too, if I could.

If it were any other night, she'd be half asleep, and I'd hear her mumble, "Keep me warm." I'd gladly do as she asked; I loved holding onto her. I loved her so much that I sometimes felt like I was floating away. I had to touch her just to bring myself back down to Earth. But she didn't ask that night—even though I knew she was freezing. That girl was too stubborn for that.

When we were twenty-two, Gen tried to get me to eat an apple, but there was a hole in it so I wouldn't do it. She spent five minutes trying to convince me that a hole in an apple don't always mean that a worm was in there. But I wasn't having it, so she took a bite and wouldn't you know it, a worm popped right out. Gen looked at me, hoping I didn't see it. But I did. I just stood there and smiled. She locked eyes with me and took another bite, like she ain't seen no worm, because there was no way she was going to admit she was wrong.

Gen and I didn't sleep much the night Lumpy died. We just lied there, in the quiet, until we heard the crows outside our window the next morning.

"Valentine's Day," Gen whispered, careful to leave out the "happy" in front of it. Her eyes were red and puffy from crying.

I sat up and groaned. "My right back hurts from that darn mattress. Right through here." I twisted so she could see what I meant.

"Rush, you don't got a right back and a left back. You got a back. And then you got a right side and a left side."

When you're with Gen, you got to get used to her correcting. No matter where you are or who you're with, even if it's s'pposed to be the holiday season. She did it to a complete stranger one Christmas when we were picking out a tree.

"This one has a nice triangular shape," the sales lady said as she lifted one of the pines from the chain link fence that it was leaning against.

I started to nod my head, because it really did have a nice triangular shape, but Gen interrupted me.

"Conical," Gen said.

The sales lady stopped brushing the snow off the branches to look at Gen.

"The word you're looking for is conical."

I'll admit that I was embarrassed at the time, but now I just laugh about it. You eventually get used to that kind of stuff after being with Gen for so long.

"Don't conical me," I said, trying to joke with her after she told me I don't got a right back. I was hoping I could get her to smile, but all I got was a screech and an ear tug out of Penny.

"I know, Baby Pens," Gen whispered as she got up to get a bottle. "We don't like Pa's stupid jokes, do we?"

I looked at the two of them. Penny was the most beautiful baby; she had hazel eyes, just like Gen. She cried a lot too. That part was 'specially like Gen.

Gen would cry and cry, and it made me realize how hard it was to love someone so much. You never want to see them sad.

"Hey," I said, "do you want to go get breakfast?"

"Not with you," she snapped.

"You ain't going to eat?"

I could have predicted her reply: "I'd rather starve than go anywhere with you." She was always the dramatic type.

"Gen, you know hoe cakes always make you feel better. Get Pens dressed. I want to take my girls to breakfast."

I had won. It was one of the few battles that I did win, but I won that one on account of Gen loving hoe cakes. That ain't nothing to brag about though, because I may've won that battle, but I was headed towards losing the war. I was going to find that out soon enough. But in the meantime, we wrapped Penny up and walked to breakfast in the cold. The warm diner air made our cheeks burn when we walked in.

Gen had agreed to go with me, but she was still giving me the cold shoulder. Lumpy's obituary was open on her phone, and she hadn't taken her eyes off it since we sat down.

I glanced at the screen. It was a full page of the nicest things you could ever read about someone. And it occurred to me that no one would ever say those kinds of things about me. What was there to write, anyways?

Rush Kilmer. Born October 31, 1983, in Fairhope, Oklahoma. Died alone on an unknown date. Disappointed everyone. Missed by no one.

I picked up some cards that were sitting at our table, hoping to fill the silence as we waited for our hoe cakes and eggs. It was one of those games for couples, to see how compatible you are.

"Let's see how we do, Gen." I was confident that we'd get a perfect score. We had always been on the same page about everything. She was my soulmate, after all.

Gen looked down at the cards and back up at me. She didn't have to say it; I knew what she was thinking.

You're touching those gross cards, and then you're going to touch your food, is what she would've said if she was talking to me. But she wasn't, so I read the first card aloud. "What's the most important thing in life?"

Gen looked at the people next to us. There was a young boy, must have only been seven or so. He was with an older couple—his grandparents, if I had to guess. They stood around the table and fumbled with some cash for the tip.

Another old man, who was sitting at a table nearby, smiled at the boy and said, "It sure is nice of a young boy to spend time with the old people."

I s'ppose it was God paying me back for all the bad things I had done in my past, if He's into such things.

Gen turned to me. "You know Penny ain't ever going to know my mama?"

"Can't we just have a nice breakfast?" I threw my napkin on the table. I about had my fill of the Oklahoma conversation.

"I'm stuck here because of you," Gen's voice cracked. A few other diners turned to look at us.

Gen's cry reminded me of a day I hadn't thought about in years. It was a day that Pa took me and Eli hunting.

Eli and I were always begging Pa to go hunting, and every once in a while, we'd come home from school on a Friday, and he'd surprise us with our hunting gear by the door. It tended to happen on the rare occasions that he was in a good mood. I know this because there'd also be less crumpled cigarette packs in the garbage.

Mama would pack us cornbread and pork because we'd be gone all weekend. She'd always put forks in our bags, too, but we'd just eat it with our fingers while we waited for the game. Mama didn't know the part about the fingers.

On the particular day that Gen reminded me of, Pa, Eli, and I were in our deer stand, licking barbeque off our hands, when a bison wandered near us. Bison move slow, and I had a clear shot. I knew he was mine.

"You're going to die, bison," I whispered as I lifted my gun.

Pa furrowed his brows, realizing that he never did teach me and Eli the most important thing about holding a life in your hands.

"Rush, that's a life. You got to be serious about it now. It's not something you can take lightly."

"Sorry, Pa," I said, but it was the kind of lip service that my mama always used to yell at me for. When you have something trapped, when you know that it's yours for the taking because it doesn't know anything about you or what you have planned, it gets real easy to forget that you're taking a life.

I looked down the rifle and looped my finger around the trigger. One little twitch of my muscle sent a bullet out of the barrel, and the bison took off running. I flew out of the deer stand and sprinted after him, following the trail of blood. He went far—out of the woods and through a field —but he didn't have much life left in him by the end. He had grown tired from the running; and the pain; and the blood loss, and he had come to rest against a large rock mound.

I stood in front of that bison, just ten feet away or so, and held my rifle steady. Pa and Eli were running across the field.

"Pa!" I yelled. "I got him!"

Pa got to the rock in time to see the bison bow his head.

"Son, back away from that bison. You listen to me, you hear?" Pa's tone was flat and stiff. I ain't ever heard him sound like that before.

"C'mon, Pa. I just need one shot."

"You listen to me, now. You can't trust a trapped animal. They're unpredictable."

I lowered my gun and walked backwards slowly, like Pa said, even though I didn't want to. Pa, Eli, and I were quiet—the only sounds were the bison's cries and the crunch of dry grass under my boots.

Gen would probably kill me if she heard me say this, but she sounded just like that trapped bison that morning in the diner, and I knew right away how she felt. Stuck, with no way out. So, I talked myself into it. I told myself that I could do it, for Gen. I said, "Gen, let's go to Oklahoma."

Her eyes lit up brighter than all the stars in the sky. "Really? Do you mean it?"

I smiled. It was good to see her so happy.

"Oh, Rush! Thank you!" she yelled as she leaned across the table to hug me, almost spilling the thick, blueberry syrup.

Gen didn't waste no time making plans. She called her mama and started searching for a house as soon as we got back from breakfast. She called High Alps and put in her two weeks. I ain't ever seen her so excited. I had my old, mint-in-a-soda Gen back.

CHAPTER 3

Victor's Basement

There's something that I thought only Pa knew about me. Well, Ricky and his girl, Georgie, knew on account of them being the ones that made me do it. It was Ricky's truck, and I only did it because Ricky said he was a good friend for never telling no one about what I did and that I owed him on that account. But it's the reason I had to run away. It's one of the secrets that I tried so hard to keep from my mama and Gen.

It was in the newspaper the next day: June 11, 2002. I came downstairs that morning, and my mama was sitting at the table with her scrambled eggs and coffee. Her eyes were as big as plates, like the not-for-eating ones with the roosters on them that she had hanging up on the wall. I knew she was already talking herself into getting her hair done, even though she went a few weeks before that, just so she could get down to the salon and hear the gossip about what she just read. She used to tell me that the salon is full of secrets that you can't find anywhere else.

When we were little, Mama would drag me and Eli to the salon once a month until I worked up the courage to ask her if we could stay home alone. It took three weeks, but I finally wore her down. She agreed to leave us home while she went to get her hair curled.

"Careful not to let the fire go out," she told us as she walked out the door.

It was by God's grace that she let us stay by ourselves, so I was not about to let God down and mess it all up by letting the fire go out. I told Eli to go get every single piece of wood that was sitting in the stack outside, because we were going to do Mama and God proud. And Eli was only six, so he carried all the wood inside, one log at a time, and he didn't know enough to say something when I started throwing it all on the fire.

After we took care of the fire, Eli and I went for a hike in the woods. Sure, we heard the sirens; we just didn't think it was for our house. But I heard my mama screaming our names. There was no mistaking that. She was louder than any sirens.

That fire climbed up the wall like it didn't want to be in the fireplace no more. My mama didn't have money to fix the house, so that corner of our living room stayed black, all the way up until the bank took the land. We weren't allowed to stay home alone no more after that fire, so Mama went back to dragging us down to the salon with her.

The salon looked just the way it did when it was built in the '70s because there wasn't any money in Fairhope. The same ladies still worked there too, and they kept styling hair the same, so all the women walked out with those bangs that flipped out around their forehead. Eli and I would sit in the sticky, pink chairs with the big, round dryers overhead—pretending like we were captured by aliens and they were trying to suck our brains out.

The ladies would sit around like hens, clucking away, but I never paid much attention to Mama's gossip, until I heard a name one day. And then that name was stuck in my head, and it stayed there and it wouldn't leave. I started wishing those dryers really could just suck my brains out because then I could forget it.

"You know that little Victor Nelson? The one that lives over there on Loomer—his pa works for the city. Well, I heard that his mama be dressing him in little girl's clothes and making him do little girl things," my mama told the other ladies.

My ears perked right up after that. I stopped watching the girl drag the broom across the linoleum so that I could concentrate on what they were saying.

"I always knew something wasn't right over there. You can tell just from looking at the house." One of the ladies put down her magazine.

"Mmmhm. It's already affecting him too." My

mama raised her eyebrows and lowered her voice. "I heard little Victor is already showing romantic interest in another little boy. The Lord ain't ever going to forgive those two."

I didn't know how to react. I didn't know how to keep my face from giving away too much. I knew a lot more than what my mama knew, but I wasn't about to tell her that.

And that's when it hit me: The Lord. I was plenty ashamed by what I did but I hadn't even considered the Lord. I sank further into my seat, hoping that the pleather would swallow me up and just praying that my mama would find something else to talk about.

Please, Mama. Please change the subject, I thought. Not that praying would have done any good anyways, seeing as how I wasn't in favor with the Lord no more.

That same thought was running through my head nine years later, on the morning of June 11, 2002, when I walked downstairs and saw my mama sitting at the table with her eggs, and her paper, and her big eyes. I kept wishing that she would just change the subject. It didn't happen though, so I guess that meant the Lord still hadn't forgiven me.

"Rush, baby, did you see this? Someone burnt up Ricky's truck!"

My heart started to beat real fast. I hated lying to my mama, but it was for her own good. It was better if she wasn't involved. Possible deniability, or something like that.

"Oh yeah?" I pretended to not know what she was talking about. Truth was, though, I knew exactly how that truck ended up on fire on that backcountry road.

It all started because Ricky lost his job. He had it pretty good down at the warehouse. It was hard work—you had to run around all day, lifting orders off the shelves, but they paid almost seven dollars an hour. That was good money for 2002, 'specially in Fairhope.

They had pretty much just one rule: don't skip the hard orders to go for an easier one. You had to do whatever's in your queue instead of throwing it back for someone else. Well, Ricky was never good at rules, so he'd always throw back the hard orders.

One day, he pulled an order for a pallet of soda. Well, that's one of the heaviest orders you can get, and Ricky was a little hungover, so he threw it back and kept throwing back the heavy ones until he got an order for a pallet of toilet paper. Ricky didn't know that the boss installed new software to tell him when people were throwing stuff back. That was Ricky's last day at the warehouse.

I was a little surprised when Ricky called me up a couple months after he got fired. We were best friends in school, but I didn't hear from him much after that because he was busy with his baby and Georgie.

"I need you to stop by," he said when I answered

the phone—not bothering to say hi or nothing, which was unusual for Ricky. He was always joking around when we were younger.

"Do you need help castrating the steers?" I asked, trying to sound upbeat, but I was groaning inside.

Castrating wasn't my fav'rite thing to do, but I was willing to do that for Ricky, because he was a good friend.

"No, I don't got steers no more. Just get here."

"Well, I'm digging holes now," I told him. I worked long hours with the telephone company, just digging and digging because when you get done with one hole there's twenty more to be dug. "I can come over after work."

"Fine. Come to Smith's," Ricky said.

"Why are you at Smith's?" I started to ask but he hung up before I could finish. When I got to Smith's, I realized why Ricky didn't want to talk about it on the phone. Ricky was living in a camper that didn't look fit for no living in. There were weeds grown up all around it, and there was a bright blue tarp over the roof to keep the weather from getting in.

It was June, so it was plenty hot inside that camper. There weren't any fans or AC. I wondered where they were bathing, because I didn't see no 'lectricity or water hook-ups, but my mama taught me that those kinds of questions ain't polite.

"I need your help with something, Rush." Ricky

was sitting at the built-in table. He kept his eyes down, like he couldn't finish asking the question if he was looking at me. He wiped at some imaginary dust on the table. "I can't afford my truck no more."

Ricky bought his truck just a few months before that. There was a rumor going around the warehouse that some of the guys were getting promoted to shift supervisor. Ricky thought he was going to be one of them, so he decided to reward himself with a nice truck. I tried to tell Ricky that he shouldn't be selling the skin before he's caught the bear, but he told me that ain't no way to live. He said that you never know the outcome if you don't take the risks.

There were about five used car lots in town, and Ricky went around to each one, trying to find the best truck there was. Georgie was so mad when she found out he paid fifteen thousand for that thing. She told Ricky that he wasn't allowed to spend no more than ten thousand, but Georgie didn't go shopping with him so she might as well have not even said it. Nothing Georgie said mattered once Ricky saw that truck. It had black paint, black rims, and a big ole V8 engine. I tried to tell Georgie that he got a pretty good deal. It was almost brand new, but she didn't care.

I didn't know what to say, though, when Ricky told me he couldn't afford his truck no more. I just sort of stood there, taking up too much space in that tiny camper.

Last I knew, Georgie was cleaning houses for a few bucks an hour. It wasn't enough to get rich on, but it was probably enough to keep them out of that camper, maybe even enough to keep Ricky's truck. I know because my mama had to do it for a while after Pa left. I thought about asking Georgie what she was doing if she wasn't cleaning, but that was another question my mama taught me to never ask a woman. I learned that one the hard way one day when my mama slapped my face before I could even finish asking, and then she needle-pointed it on a pillow for good measure.

I took out my wallet. I think there was about one hundred dollars in there at the time. It wasn't much, but I tried to offer it to Ricky anyways.

"I don't make much digging holes, so this all I have," I told him.

Ricky pushed the crumpled-up bills towards me. "I'm in deeper than that. I need to get rid of the truck."

"Why don't you just sell it, then?" It seemed like a no-brainer to me.

"Don't you think I tried that, Rush?" Ricky slammed his fist on the table, and the baby started crying. Georgie made a face at Ricky and got up to go quiet the baby. "I tried, but it ain't worth what I have on the loan," Ricky said, softer this time.

"What are you going to do?" I wiped at the sweat that had started to pool on my forehead.

"When I bought the car, the guy talked me into buying gap insurance. It covers the difference between what my car's worth and what I owe the bank. But they only pay if something happens to your car, like an accident or something."

Ricky and I just stared at each other. It was like he was waiting for me to put the pieces together, but I was never good at puzzles. Gen said it was because I didn't start with the edge pieces.

"Now, before you say no, I want you to remember that I know your secret," he warned me.

I looked over at Georgie, making sure she didn't hear Ricky, but she was still busy with the baby.

"Before I say no to what, Ricky?" I whispered, hoping he'd start to do the same.

"Before you say no to helping me pretend it was stolen."

This is the point in the conversation where my eyes just about popped out of my head. There was no way I was going to help Ricky steal his truck. He had crossed a line that time. Sure, I used to go fishing with Ricky, even though we didn't have no license. But this wasn't some misdemeanor that he was talking about. He was talking about committing a felony.

"Sorry, man," I said as I got up to leave.

"Wait, Rush." Ricky stood up, too. "I'll give you two percent of what I get from the insurance company."

I told Ricky that two percents ain't a lot of percents, but he explained that it added up to a lot when you take two percent of a big number. It'd be three hundred dollars, he told me.

I thought about it for a moment. Three hundred was almost two weeks of work. Two weeks of digging hole after hole. It was tempting, but no amount of money was going to make me do that. (I later realized that it would be zero percents given that all his insurance money went to the loan.)

I didn't need to make things worse between me and God, anyhow. I told Ricky that I didn't want nothing to do with it.

"Fine. I guess you don't think it's fair to help me after I've helped you by keeping your secret all these years," he replied.

One time, Gen asked me what my biggest secret was. I told her the first thing that came to my mind; I told her that I can't sleep without a blanket that I've had since I was little and that I like to press it to my face from time to time. That was all true—I really did have a blanket, and I really did like to smell it, but that wasn't my biggest secret. I had two 'big' secrets: one was about Ricky's truck, and the other, well, there was no way that I could tell Gen about that one either. But I guess now is as good a time as any to come clean. So here it is:

When I was eight, my mama handed me a big box of candy and shoved me out the door. The dust was thick outside and the box was heavy, but I had to get those bars sold so that I could win one of the prizes from the school. I had my eye on one of those cassette players. All I had to do was sell about firty of those milk chocolate bars. Now, before you ask—firty is somewhere between thirty and forty—another thing Gen always hated. But you ask any other Okie: Firty is as much of a number as the rest of them.

"It doesn't make no sense," Gen would say. "Thirty is the smaller number, so it'd have to come first. Like thorty."

"Thorty? Well that's just plain dumb-sounding," I told her.

So, I had firty or so chocolate bars to sell, and my mama pushed me out the door and told me to get to getting. Mama believed in treating kids like adults, so she sent me on my way.

"Make sure you're back by dinner. Don't make me come looking for you," she called out to me from the screen door.

I managed to sell one of those 'spensive bars to almost every house on the street. I was fancying myself a bit of a salesman as I walked up to the next house. I didn't know who lived there, but I didn't think much of it. I didn't know who lived in most of the houses that I sold chocolate to, anyways.

I rang the doorbell and counted how many bars I had left. *Two, four, six, eight, ten, twelve.*

I wasn't scared at the time, because I didn't yet know that twelve was bad for me. But this is when it all began. This is when the number *twelve* started showing up every single time something bad was going to happen.

"Hello?" A boy answered the door. He was my age, but I didn't recognize him. He wasn't in my class at school or nothing. I would have remembered his hair for sure. It was almost down to his shoulders. You got to remember that this was 1992—before guys were walking around with those buns on top of their heads. Most kids my age had the type of hair your mama gave you when she stuck a bowl on your head at the kitchen table.

There was a woman standing behind the boy. A lady whose name I later learned was Jonetta Nelson. Now, Jonetta's face did look familiar. She reminded me of that week Eli ran away, when my mama didn't sleep the entire time. She had the same dark circles that this lady did. I didn't think much of it, though. I just fig'red that this boy had that same bad streak that Eli had. Boy, did Eli give our mama a hard time. He was only six at that point, but he was always harassing the neighbor's chickens and staying out past dinner. If this boy was anything like Eli, it was no wonder this woman looked so tired.

"I'm selling chocolate for school," I said as I held out the box. It was my signature move, a rule that had proven true at each door I knocked on: The closer chocolate is to your face, the more likely you are to grab it.

The boy started to reach for one, but Jonetta pulled his hand away.

"No, sorry. We're not interested." She looked me up and down a couple times. "What's your name?"

"Rush Bernard Kilmer," I said proudly. I can hear

Gen now, snorting at my lowly three names.

"Well, hey, I have an idea. Do you want to come inside for some lemonade? Victor, here, might be able to find a game for you two to play." She put her hand on his skinny shoulder. It almost looked like she was digging her fingers into his collarbone, but I fig'red I must have been imagining things.

See, now, I was an eight-year-old boy, so of course I agreed to lemonade and games and followed them inside. They didn't have a lot of furniture, maybe a wicker chair or two, but that was pretty typical décor in Fairhope.

I can't blame them for being poor, because Mama, Eli, and I were poor as dirt. But Mama taught me and Eli to be God-fearing people. We had cheap sheets that were thin and rough, but they were pulled tight against the mattress each morning. And our lace curtains had yellowed over the years, but they were always drawn to let the light in.

Jonetta's house was nothing like that. It looked like they didn't want no one seeing what they were doing inside, including God. There was cardboard covering every inch of their windows.

I asked, just like any young boy without manners might've done, "Why are all your windows covered, ma'am?"

She smirked, as if that was just about the silliest question that she could think of. "Dust, dear," she said simply. I nodded like I understood.

I followed Jonetta into the kitchen and pulled myself onto a wooden stool at the counter. Victor picked at the laminate that was peeling from the sticky cabinets as Jonetta grabbed a bag of powder and swirled spoonfuls into two glasses of water.

"Here you go: my special lemonade. Be careful with the cups, now," she said as she handed us the glasses.

To this day, I still ain't sure what made it her special lemonade, but Victor and I gulped it as we walked down the hall to his room. I was expecting his room to be like the rest of the house, dark and empty. But it wasn't. The walls were bright pink. At first, I thought maybe it was his sister's hand-me-down room. I remember that Ricky got his sister's hand-me-down room when she moved to the basement, and it was pink until his mama saved up enough money to paint it. But then Victor opened a plastic tub that had even more pink stuff: teddy bears, dolls, the kinds of things that I always planned on buying for Pens when she got older.

"What's your sister's name?" I asked him.

"I don't got one," he replied, without really looking at me. I could tell he was ashamed of the stuff.

I tried to change the subject. "How come I never seen you at school before?"

"I'm homeschooled. My mama taught me how to use an eyelash curler today." Victor held a piece of rubber-coated metal to his eye.

"Is that for when you're bad?" I asked, nodding my head like I knew what he was talking about. My mama would just get Pa's old belt out, but I thought maybe they didn't have no belts to spare. I imagined Jonetta dragging him around the room by that thing if he didn't come home in time for dinner.

"No, it's not for punishing. It's for making your eyelashes curly," he told me.

I ain't ever heard of wanting to make your eyelashes curly before then, but I knew my mama was always trying to make her hair curly, so it seemed like it'd be something for girls. I started to wonder if homeschool was something only girls did, maybe to learn how to be more girly. It made sense to me. I fig'red it wouldn't do them no good to learn no math and science in real school anyhow.

Victor mumbled something and pulled two dolls out of the plastic tub.

I never had no interest in playing with dolls, so I stuck my hand in my pocket and showed him my two toy cars. Pa gave them to me for my birthday one year. We spent that entire day zooming those things around the floor. Besides hunting, it was one of our fav'rite things to do together. I always kept the cars in my pocket, hoping that he'd come back and want to play with me again one day.

Victor's eyes lit up when he saw them. I had never seen someone so happy about toy cars. He grabbed the little green coupe from my hand, and we zoomed those cars across the shaggy, brown carpet. I was the sheriff, and he was driving the getaway car.

"Wee—ooh—wee—ooh," I did my best to make the siren noise. We were having a blast until Jonetta walked in.

"Vick—" Jonetta stopped mid-sentence when she saw us. "What's going on here?"

Victor tightened his fist around the car. I wasn't sure if he was trying to hide it from her or just keep her from taking it. "We, we were just—," he stuttered.

Jonetta stomped over to him and peeled his fingers back, one by one. She plucked the car from his hand and then demanded mine too.

"Basement. Now," she ordered.

"But, Mama—"

"Now!" she screamed. "And tell your friend that he can either come with us or he has to go home."

Victor turned to me. He was quiet for a second. "Do you want to come?" he asked meekly.

I shrugged my shoulders, not really sure what I was agreeing to, but curiosity got the better of me.

Victor and I followed her into the basement. It was dark, except for a thin stream of light that was coming in from the small, cinderblock windows. The damp, musty smell made me cough.

I reached for the light switch, but Jonetta's hand stung my skin. She looked up into the basement rafters like she was waiting for something to come down. I looked up there too, but I didn't see nothing but cobwebs.

Thick rolls of ins'lation hung like bodies from the ceiling cavities, as if someone had pulled them from the joists in search of something. I guess I should have turned around right then, but I just kept following them deeper into the basement.

Victor knelt in front of another plastic tub and pulled out two pink dresses. They had all sorts of ribbons and bows on them. He threw one in my direction and then turned his back to me as he slowly stepped into the other.

"Vickie, darling, come here and let me fix your hair," Jonetta said.

When Victor was done getting dressed, he sat down in front of Jonetta on the cold, cement floor. She took handfuls of his hair and wrapped it around a hot iron. Steam came off the metal, just the same as it did when my mama did it to her own hair. When she was finished with the iron, Victor's mama coated his head in hairspray, until the whole basement was sticky and tasted like chemicals. That's when I realized why his hair was so long.

"Have a seat, everyone. Thank you all for coming." Jonetta gestured to a small, wood table with kid-sized chairs. "I know the weather is just frightful today, what with the dust and all."

She set glass teacups on the table and pretended to pour something in them. Victor reached for his cup, but his knuckle grazed the handle. The glass shattered against the concrete.

Victor froze, his arm hanging there mid-air, like

a marionette's might if the puppeteer had forgotten what was next in the skit.

I don't think Victor had forgotten, though. I think he knew exactly what was to come. All the color had drained from his face.

The puppeteer suddenly remembered the arm, hanging there mid-air, and he set it down on top of Victor's other arm. Victor started picking again, but this time, it was the skin on the back of his hand. He picked feverishly, until raw flesh appeared and blood trickled down the sides.

He stared at Jonetta, but she didn't say a word. Instead, she stood up from the table and walked straight upstairs. She wasn't a heavy woman, but the basement stairs creaked under her weight. We sat in silence as we listened to her footsteps on the floor above us. The basement stairs creaked once more, and then she was standing by the shattered cup with a piece of bread and a hammer in her hands.

"Do you know how hard it is to get up all these shards?" she asked as she began pressing the bread against the concrete floor. "This is the only way to get them all."

"Mama, no! Anything but that! Please!" Victor cried.

Jonetta stood up and calmly set the bread down in front of Victor. She stood in front of him, towering over his small body, until he brought the bread to his mouth and took bite after bite. My stomach turned as I heard the glass crunch between his teeth, and no matter how hard I tried, I couldn't stop myself from picturing the glass shredding his tongue and throat into a stringy mess.

I felt myself relax a little when Victor had finished the bread. My shoulders fell. My breathing had returned to almost-normal. I thought the worst was over.

It wasn't.

"Hands on the table," Jonetta said.

We were afraid of what might happen if we didn't listen—well, I was anyway. Victor was probably afraid of what he *knew* would happen if we didn't listen, so we quickly set our hands on the table. Jonetta adjusted my hands so that the space between them was just wide enough to fit a plastic car, and she did the same to Victor's. Then, she set my toy cars in the spaces that she so carefully created.

Jonetta pulled her hands away for a moment, but then tweaked the cars so that they were perfectly parallel between our thumbs. When she was satisfied with the angles of everything, she grabbed the hammer and raised it by her head, aiming it in my direction. I wasn't sure if she was trying for my fingers or the car, and I didn't know which one I was worried about more. Those cars meant everything to me.

I winced and closed my eyes. When I opened them, I saw my green coupe, smashed to bits. My heart broke into just as many pieces.

She turned towards Victor and raised the hammer again. My heart raced as I reached for the red sports car. I was willing to risk every bone in my fingers to save that car, but I was too late. The hammer came down on the car, and I started to cry some more. My pa would've got out the belt and gave me a few whippings for crying so much over a car. Victor's mama didn't pay me no mind, though. She just wiped the pieces on the floor and reached for a fake biscuit, which was s'pposed to be our signal to carry on with the tea party.

Victor copied her movements. As he reached across the table, the sleeve of his shirt pulled up, and I noticed a bruise that I didn't see before. If I had seen it earlier, I might've thought it was from falling from a tree or crashing a bike, normal boy stuff, but now I wasn't so sure.

I reached for a fake biscuit too, careful to avoid the remaining dishware. I held it in my hand as Victor and Jonetta chomped away on air. I guess you could say that I was in shock because I couldn't do anything but sit there.

Jonetta rubbed her hands together to shake off the 'crumbs,' and then pulled a large book out from under the table. I noticed that the dark blue cover wasn't dusty, just like the table and the plastic tub weren't dusty. That wasn't how the rest of the basement looked, though; I could barely tell what color the washer and dryer were s'pposed to be.

I caught a glimpse of the book's title as Jonetta flipped through the pages: *Love Poems of the Cen-*

tury.

"Vickie, read this poem to Rush." She set the book on the table when she found one that she liked.

Victor was obedient. He took the book without so much as a sideways glance.

"My dearest love," he began.

"No! No! No!" She slammed the book out of his hands. "Say it like you mean it, or I'll get the sand again."

I wasn't sure what she was going to do with the sand, but it seemed like it wasn't something Victor wanted her to do because he started the poem again. His voice was softer than the last time.

"My dearest love—how long I've wanted to touch your skin, to kiss your lips, to be near your beating heart. My heart is beating, too. It beats for you and only you."

Jonetta must have been pleased with his performance that time because she sat quietly with a smile.

"Now hold hands," she instructed.

Victor looked at me, a mix of permission and apology, I guess, before wrapping his fingers around mine. That was when I started feeling guilty about what we were doing. I was a boy, and Victor was a boy, no matter how much Jonetta wanted to believe otherwise. I knew my mama wouldn't forgive me. But I was also scared of Jonetta, and I was scared for Victor, so I just kept doing what Jonetta told us to do. I kept waiting for it to get better.

The weird thing is that I don't remember anything after that. It was like I blacked out. The next memory I have is being back at my mama's house, talking to Ricky on the phone.

I wish I could say that was the last time I went down there, but it wasn't. I kept going back to Victor's house. I don't know why I went back. I don't know if I kept expecting there to be something different, or if I was just plain curious about the things Jonetta did.

But it all started out the same. We'd drink lemonade, we'd go down to the basement, and then everything would go black. I told Ricky about it each time because he was my best friend. He said he'd never tell a soul. And he didn't, but I guess I was to pay him back for that.

CHAPTER 4

Ricky's Truck

Committing fraud just ain't the kind of thing you get up and do. I didn't know that, though, cause I ain't ever done anything like that before. So, when Ricky reminded me that he had kept my secret all those years, I fig'red okay then, fair's fair. I headed towards the camper's door, planning on getting to work. I was always the kind of person that would just get up and do things when I had a mind to.

"Sit down, man. It's not even dark out," Ricky threw his arm at the window. "And we have to fig're out a plan, anyways."

"I thought we were pretending someone stole it," I said.

Ricky looked at me like he was second-guessing his decision to pick me as his partner. I s'ppose he would have picked someone smarter if they had owed him a favor too. I was all he had, though, so he was going to try to make it work.

"We need an alibi. I was thinking that we'll head down to Moe's. Order some drinks. Let people see us," he said.

"What kind of drinks?" I asked, considering all the different choices. "Even within beer itself, you got ale, pale ale, India pale ale, brown ale—I, personally, prefer a strong, dry stout—"

"It don't goddamn matter, Rush." He slammed his fist on the table. "After you order, go to the bathroom and slip out of the window so the cameras can't see you. You're skinny enough; you'll fit."

I thought it over for a second. It seemed like as good a plan as any. I certainly wasn't going to come up with anything better, and Ricky seemed to have it all fig'red out. With all of Ricky's pre-planning, I thought there was no way we'd get in trouble.

So, I hung around that camper until the sun went down. Ricky, Georgie and I played poker, and I lost every single penny that I put in. That was how it always went for me—I was never any good at poker. I had no idea why at the time, but now I know. Turns out, I was no good at reading people. Never did have that skill; I always took people for their word. I wanted to find the good in people, I guess.

After I lost all my money to Ricky and Georgie, Ricky told me not to worry about it. He told me that he'd buy me a beer at the bar since I couldn't afford it no more. He didn't tell me what kind of beer, as he was still insisting that it didn't matter, but he made it sound like he was doing me a favor. I wasn't so sure. I felt like I was the one doing the favors.

When it got dark, me, Ricky, and Georgie dropped the baby off with Smith and headed down to Moe's. Moe's was a terrible place for being. It'd break my mama's heart if she knew I went there. It was where all the no-goods went to forget about their no-good doings of the day. I used to consider myself better than them, but I guess we are all the same now.

We pulled into the parking lot, and I counted the cars. It was a habit by then, to count. It had become as second nature as breathing.

Two, four, six, eight, ten, twel—

"We got to turn around, Ricky. We can't be here," I said as I cut the wheel and started speeding towards the parking lot exit. The truck bounced on the gravel.

"Get a grip, Rush. You can't back out now. You already said you were going to help me," Ricky shot back. He reached for the steering wheel.

Every piece of me knew that I should turn around. Every piece of me knew that this wasn't going to end well, but I listened to Ricky anyhow. I guess I had a habit of doing that over the years.

I parked the truck, and the three of us walked inside. I took a seat next to a hunched-over ball of flannel that had his forehead resting on his arm.

I startled him when I sat down, and he glanced up long enough for me catch the gritty sawdust in the wrinkles on his face. My pa was a logger, so I'd recognize that dust anywhere.

"How are you doing?" I asked him.

He gave me a small nod, like he didn't want to give me the time of day. But since I had already made him lift his head from his forearm, he took that opportunity to take another gulp of whiskey. As he drained the glass, I caught sight of another thing that I'd know anywhere: a tiny, black, cross tattoo on the inside of his right wrist.

"P-Pa?" I managed to get out. I was half-afraid to know the answer.

The man turned to me and squinted. "Eli?"

I was a little hurt that he didn't recognize me, but I couldn't blame him for thinking I was Eli. I guess I didn't look like no twelve-year-old boy no more. And I wouldn't have recognized him either, if it weren't for that tattoo. He didn't look like the strong, healthy man that I knew all those years ago.

"It's me, Rush," was all I managed to say, even though I had seven years to prepare. I had played it out so many times in my head, imagining what I'd say to him. Some days, I imagined telling him how angry I was that he left me, Mama, and Eli. I'd tell him all about how Mama couldn't afford to run the farm by herself and about the day that sheriff stuck the bright pink foreclosure sign on our window. Everyone in Fairhope knew exactly what that pink sticker meant. You didn't even have to be close enough to read it.

I was going to tell Pa how embarrassed we were when we became the salon's gossip, and I was going to tell him all about the tiny, one-bedroom trailer that we had to move in to. Mama slept on the couch so that Eli and I could have the bed. I wanted him to feel all the pain I felt over the past seven years.

Other days, though, I just imagined wrapping my arms around him and never letting ago. I swore that I'd never let him out of my sight again so that he couldn't run away no more. I was going to tell him how much I missed him and how sorry I was if I was the reason he left.

I used to think he left because I kept forgetting to turn the barn lights off when I was done feeding the animals. Pa would yell at me over and over about how we couldn't afford to be wasting no 'lectricity.

"We're hundreds of thousands of dollars in debt! Don't you realize we're *this* close to losing the farm?" he'd yell. And when I still didn't listen, he'd get too mad for words and throw whatever was in his hand, usually a shovel or a pitchfork. Mama said that there wasn't anything anyone can do that would make someone deserve to have a shovel thrown at them, but Pa didn't think so.

And when that still didn't work, he'd pull my pants down and whip my bare butt.

"Spare the rod, spoil the child," he'd say.

No amount of beatings ever could make me remember, though, and I thought maybe he left because he was just tired of dealing with me. Mama told me that it wasn't my fault, but I'm not sure I ever fully believed her.

I had spent so long playing out those conversations in my head, but I couldn't go through with either of them when I saw him in the bar. Too shocked, I guess. I just kept staring at him. A million questions were running through my head.

"Why did you leave us?" I blurted. I s'ppose it sounded more accusatory than I intended. Maybe that's what pissed him off. But I just genuinely wanted to know. It had eaten at me for almost seven years, and it came out of my mouth before I could rethink it.

He looked ashamed, but not surprised, like he knew it was coming.

"Fear. I've been running for a long time," he told his whiskey glass, like it was the whiskey who he left sitting on the porch step as he pulled from our driveway onto Route 58 for the last time.

"Well, how long you been back?" I asked.

"Not long, I s'ppose. How have, uh, your mama and Eli been?" He stuttered through their names, as if he couldn't recall them at first.

"Mama never got hitched if that's what you're wondering. Never even went out on a date. And Eli is doing real good on the football team."

"And how you been, boy?"

Me. I wanted to think he saved the best for last.

There was something about his voice that made me melt into that same little boy again. The one that would run to his pa to make everything better. I really needed that, what with all that was going on with Ricky and the truck, so I lowered my voice and told him everything. I told him about Victor and the basement. I told him about how I had to pay Ricky back now. I told him our whole plan for getting Ricky that gap money. A wave of relief fell over me after I had gotten all of it out.

Pa didn't say nothing at first. I knew he wanted to be disappointed in me. I knew it. But I also knew that he didn't have any room to say anything based on how he chose to live his own life.

"Well, you just be careful," was all he said.

"That's it?"

I was hoping he'd say more. I was hoping he'd tell me what to do to make it all better. I didn't want to burn no truck, but I felt like I didn't have no choice. I didn't want Ricky to tell no one about what I did.

"What do you want me to say?"

"Well, should I do what Ricky says?"

"You're a grown man, son. I can't make your decisions for you no more. It'll turn out one way or the other." Pa set his glass down and gripped my shoulder. "Listen, can you do something for me?"

He made it sound so simple, like he wanted me to pick him up a pack of smokes on the way home like I used to. I nodded my head, ready to do almost anything to win him back.

"I got myself into some trouble, and there's only one way that I can see myself out of it. I just wanted you to know that I'm sorry. Think you can forgive me?"

"Of course, Pa," I said. I had no idea what he was talking about, but I nodded my head eagerly—trying to show him that I didn't care about whatever he had done.

He gave my shoulder a pat, and then he walked out of my life, just like that. The bar door swung behind him, and I never saw him again. I wondered if I should've made it seem like Mama, Eli and I needed him a little bit more. Like we were falling apart without him. Or maybe Pa just lost the nerve to face Mama and Eli after leaving them in the Oklahoma dust all those years ago. Or, the one that haunted me the most: Maybe I had disappointed him for the second, and final, time in my life.

Ricky turned to me once Pa was gone. "Who was that?" he asked.

"I don't know," I told him, which was the truth. He wasn't the man I knew back then.

"Well good job working on that alibi. That guy can vouch for us now."

"Yeah, I guess," I said, knowing that no one was ever going to find Pa if Pa didn't want to be found.

"You ready?" Ricky asked me.

I wasn't, but I got up out of the seat and walked towards the bathroom anyways. The rest of the details are fuzzy because the stout had hit me hard, and my head just wasn't in it anymore. I kept replaying my conversation with Pa.

But I guess I did everything the way Ricky told me to. I do remember wiping the truck down with bleach, on account of how strong that smell was. And I remember holding a bright blue bottle of 'celerant and the smell of sulfur from the matches. It felt like only thirty minutes had gone by when I found myself back in the bar again, sitting next to Ricky and Georgie. I should've been more careful—more aware of what I was doing, but all I could think about was Pa.

"Did you clean it up good?" Ricky asked me when I got back to the bar.

I nodded my head.

When Ricky got home that night, he called his insurance company and told them that someone gone and stole his truck. He was happy as a clam, thinking that the night had gone off without a hitch. He told the insurance company the story that he cooked up. He told them that I asked him if he wanted to go have a little fun that night. He said that I got to his house and picked him up in my truck. That we had a few drinks and stayed until the bar closed at two o'clock, and then I drove him home, and that's when he saw the truck was missing.

Ricky thought that he'd get a check in the mail in the next day or so but the insurance company wasn't so sure. They wanted to ask Ricky more questions. They wanted to talk to me. They wanted to see our cell phone records and Ricky's bank account.

"What do they want to talk to me for?" I asked Ricky after I got a phone call from the investigator.

"They said our stories don't make no sense," he replied through bites of food. He didn't seem the least bit concerned that we were headed for jail.

I tried to be more like Ricky and less like me. I went about my business for the next two days, telling myself that this was no big deal. Finally, it was June 13th: the day I was s'pposed to meet the investigator in a conference room at the Fairhope motel.

I was in a bad mood when I woke up that morning. I picked a fight with Eli over where he left his shoes in the hall, and I snubbed the pancakes my mama made us for breakfast. I thought about skipping the meeting, but then they'd for sure know I was guilty. I fig'red my best chance was to go along with their questions, like I ain't got nothing to hide. All I had to do was stick with Ricky's story. Ricky said that if I stuck with the story, I'd be fine.

I opened the heavy motel door and was greeted by the receptionist. She smiled at me, because she didn't know me or what I had done, and she pointed me towards Conference Room B. I was scared out of my skin walking into that room. There was a guy in a suit, waiting for me at a big, glossy table. A tape recorder sat in the center.

"Hello Mr. Kilmer." The man pressed the red button on the recorder and motioned for me to take a seat. The tape started spinning. "I'm going to record our conversation about Richard Beaumont's insurance claim. Do you understand what under oath means, Mr. Kilmer?"

"Yes, sir." I sat down. The leather was cold against my sweaty back.

"And do you solemnly swear that you will tell the truth, the whole truth, and nothing but the truth, so help you God, under pains and penalties of perjury?"

Perjury. I had never heard that word before. *Perjury. Per a jury? Is that whatever a jury decides? What is a hung jury, anyhow?*

"Yes, sir," I blurted, suddenly realizing I had taken too long to answer him.

"Please state your name for the record and then describe what happened the night of June the 10th."

"My name is, uh, Rush Kilmer." I tried to remember what Ricky said so we could match. "I had just worked a long day, and I went over Ricky's place because he called me."

"He called you?"

Shoot. I had already messed up once, so I thought I'd better bring up Pa. Ricky said that details make lies look like truths.

"No. I mean, I called him. And then I picked him up, and we went to Moe's. When we got to the bar, I saw my pa. We talked for a while, and then I dropped Ricky back off at home."

"You were at the bar the entire night?" The man raised his eyebrows at me.

"Yes, sir."

"Was anyone else with you?"

"No," I said, not wanting to drag Georgie into this mess.

"Rush, we got a tip that you may've had something to do with the theft. Do you know anything about that?"

My heart sank. Only three people knew that: Ricky, Georgie, and Pa. I didn't think Ricky and Georgie would tell on account of them being involved.

"No, sir."

"Alright. That's all we need today, Mr. Kilmer. I'm sure that we'll be in touch." The man nodded his head instead of shaking my hand.

I got the feeling that he didn't believe me, but I tried to shrug it off. Ricky told me that this was a fool-proof plan and that there was no way we were going to get in trouble. But then Ricky called me later that day, and I knew my life was over.

"Is you interested in knowing what I know?" Ricky's voice sounded slick, almost like he was smiling. "The insurance company knows you lied to them. They think you stole my truck because you were mad at me. They're coming after you."

"What? Why would they think that?" I asked him.

"I don't know, Rush. I told them that we played

poker and that I took you for the only hundred that you had. They asked if you were at the bar the whole night, and I told them that there were a few hours where you were gone. I guess they put two and two together and four makes you look real guilty."

"Why'd you go and tell them that I was gone?" I was stunned. It didn't seem like Ricky was looking out for me no more. For a second, I wondered if he was the tipster.

"They send you to jail for telling fibs. What was I s'pposed to say?"

"Maybe they'll go easy on us if we confess," I said to Ricky, but mostly, I was just talking aloud. My mind raced.

"Don't you say nothing to no one." Ricky's tone changed, from slick to angry. "You got to run, Rush. Go to Silverheel, Montana. There are laws on paper but there ain't no laws in real life. The sheriff don't care about nothing there, so ain't no one going to hunt you down in Silverheel. Oh, and one more thing—don't ever come back to Fairhope." And then Ricky hung up the phone.

I ain't proud of it, but for the second time in two days, I did what Ricky said. I didn't think I had much other choice. That was the day I packed my truck up and kissed my mama goodbye. She cried and cried at the kitchen table when I told her that I was leaving. I think she did just about everything she could've to get me to stay.

"I know how much you hate digging those holes

day in and day out. I can pick up a third job and take care of the both of us," she pleaded. "Maybe we can get some loans, and you can go to college."

I studied her face and noticed, for the first time, just how the years had started to wear on her skin. I tried to memorize every line and every freckle, knowing that I'd never see her again. That thought was almost too much to bear. I turned to push the door open so that she wouldn't see the tears in my eyes.

I told myself that leaving was for the better. I had graduated almost a year prior, and I was still living at home. Whenever someone would ask about me, my mama would say, "Rush is still living at home, but he's a hard-working boy." She always had to put the *but* in there to make up for the fact that I was still in her house.

I swung my frayed duffle bag onto my shoulder and stood there for a second, waiting for her to say goodbye, but she didn't say nothing. That was when she came running after me, asking me why she's not enough to make me stay, and I told her some story about how I needed to see new places.

I drove to Silverheel and never looked back. She called me once a week after that. On Sundays after dinner, like clockwork. I never did answer though. I couldn't handle hearing her voice. Leaving her altogether was easier than leaving a part of her.

I guess she didn't see it that way, but I reckon none of it matters no more. She died in 2012, about ten years after I left. The same year that

Pens was born. Eli clipped her obituary out of the paper and mailed it to me. Didn't say nothing else. Just stuck that obituary in an envelope and shipped it off. I guess he was mad at me for breaking her heart.

And there I was, ready to break Gen's heart too. It made me angry that I kept doing that, like I didn't know how to do anything else with my life. I loved Gen, just as much as I loved my mama. I didn't have a second chance to make things right with Mama, but I still had time to make things right with Gen. I wanted to do better this time around.

So, I was feeling real good about myself when I decided to tell Gen that we were going back. Seeing her so happy at the diner made it all worth it. I was dreading telling Ricky though. I sort of fig'red he wasn't going to be thrilled about it.

We didn't time breakfast right, so when we got back home, Penny was about an hour past due for a nap. She screamed and arched in Gen's arms. Normally, Gen would've been frustrated with Penny at this point, but she was so happy about going back to Oklahoma that the smile didn't leave her face.

Once Gen had left the room to put Penny down for nap, I slipped my phone out of my pocket. I hesitated for a second, but I knew I had to tell Ricky I was coming home. It was just a matter of time before he saw me back in Fairhope anyhow.

Plus, Ricky committed more crimes than I ever

did, and he was still living in Fairhope. So, I told him that I was coming back because it was what Gen wanted. I barely had time to put my phone away before he replied:

You know what will happen if you do.

I tried to reason with him, fig'ring he was a reasonable person. It had been a while since the whole truck thing, so I was hoping that Ricky and I could let bygones go on by:

That was a long time ago.
Ain't no one going to come after me now, Ricky.

You can't ever come back, Rush.
That was the deal.

You don't understand.
Gen won't live in Montana no more.
I have to come back.

You'll regret it.
I promise.

For once, I was grateful that Penny would put up a fight at nap time. I was never good at thinking on my feet, and I needed that time to come up with a plan.

I heard Gen "shush, shush" and "there, there" until, finally, Penny was in her crib sleeping peacefully, wholly unaware of what was about to happen between me and Gen.

Gen sat down next to me on the couch, in a sort

of leap-and-plop that a kid might do after you've given her too much sugar. She held out her phone to show me a house that was for sale in Fairhope.

The paint was peeling from the wood siding, and it was missing almost half of its round, clay shingles. Only the door, which was painted bright teal, seemed like it was cared for. The realtor used creative words like "cozy" and "fixer-upper."

There were a few trees around the house, but nothing else. It sat in the middle of a dead, flat field. It was everything that I left all those years ago—everything that I could never go back to.

"It's seventy thousand, but I fig're we can make the mortgage if we just—" Gen started to say.

"Listen, Gen," I interrupted, "I was thinking it over, and I like my job. I want to stay."

Her jaw fell. "What are you talking about?"

"It's done. I made up my mind. I'm not talking about this no more," I said before standing up and walking to the kitchen.

I scooped some instant coffee into a mug and clinked the spoon against the ceramic as I swirled those grinds around, trying to drown out Gen's sobs from the other room. She was crying rivers—lakes, even. Enough to fill Lake Panguitch, I'd reckon.

CHAPTER 5

Gen's Wheels

Gen eventually stopped crying, and I thought everything had blown over by the next morning. Well, as much as anything could blow over with Gen, anyways. I used to get over things real quick, but she liked to hold onto them—she held onto them tighter than any valuables she had. She never did find her gold-plated earrings or her other set of car keys. But you can bet that she remembered the time that I only made coffee for myself and didn't ask her if she wanted any. She remembered it every day—every time she saw the coffee maker or our blue ceramic mugs.

So, I s'ppose I shouldn't have been surprised when I saw that she was still mad at me for going back on my word. That was pretty much to be expected those days. I couldn't give her what she wanted, and she thought that I wasn't being fair about it. I fig'red she'd come around eventually, though. It was just a matter of time. I just had to wait it out until the snow thawed. When the snow thawed, Gen would thaw.

It was February 15th, so I had nearly four more months to go until summer. Then, we could get back to how we were before. We could sleep by the river and whisper to each other in the dark. It would be me, her, and Pens—every night, for the rest of our lives.

The mountains are dangerous, a lot more dangerous than any plains. It takes a special set of skills to survive out there, so I had already set my mind to teach Pens how to protect herself. I was going to teach her to swim and track animals so that she'd be the kind of baby that can take care of herself in the mountains.

I was feeling pretty good about my own survival skills. I had a book about what kind of plants you can eat in the wild (always avoid ones with milky sap), I knew how to catch a fish with my bare hands, and I could make a shelter out of just about anything you gave me. And I thought I had the people part down, too, seeing how I took care of Kenny and Art. I thought I could make it out there. I feel pretty stupid for thinking that now, but at the time, I had no clue, so I set out to win Gen over.

I started doing everything I could think of just to get us to summer. I jumped up as soon as Pens was awake so that Gen wouldn't have to, even though it was five in the morning and I wanted nothing more than to keep sleeping. I even put some bait near the hole in the wall where the ants were getting in.

Gen asked me to patch the hole. She thought I was being lazy by just putting some bait down, but I had a plan. I was planning on learning the enemy. You can beat any enemy if you just sit and watch them. Everyone has a routine, and every routine has a weakness. I planned to spend most of that day just sitting there, watching the ants, studying their patterns.

I learned that ants are lazy. They don't come out until around noon or so.

By around one o'clock, the colony had sent all their resources to that bait, probably thinking that it was the best thing ever. That was a lesson that I wish I would've learned sooner, because I was making that same mistake at the time. I was putting all my resources into saving something that was working against me. I just didn't know it yet.

So, after I had set my mind to smoothing things over with Gen, but before I had fully understood the lesson that could've been learned from the ants, I was in the kitchen, cooking Gen some hoe cakes for a late lunch. Hoe cakes ain't nothing special—just some cornmeal and milk, fried on the griddle until golden-brown—but Gen was a helpless thing in the kitchen.

She always said that my hoe cakes were the best she ever had. "Better than the restaurants," she'd brag to her mama. Gen used to say that I was the best cook in the world.

"You've never even been out of the country," I'd argue.

"I don't need to," she'd assure me with a kiss on the cheek.

At the time, I knew Gen hadn't seen the whole world, maybe just a few states besides Oklahoma and Montana. Now, though? Who knows? I've been missing for more than seven years. I have no idea where she is or what she's doing. Maybe she finally did get to see the whole world.

I've never been much of a traveler myself, despite what I told my mama that day I left Oklahoma. But I think I would have liked to be a chef if I had done some things differently, made some different choices. Not one of those fancy chefs in New York City or anything like that, but maybe I could have owned a small diner in Silverheel. That just wasn't meant to be, I guess, because the only person I ever cooked for was Gen. Not that I minded it much at the time because I loved her more than anything.

So, there I was, mixing hoe cake batter for Gen when the house phone rang. Right away, I was surprised because ain't no one ever call us on the house phone. The only reason we had the darn thing was because the cable company said it'd lower our bill if we bundled. I never did understand how that worked but Gen was the one who handled all the bills so she bundled right up.

Since no one ever called us on that line, I just let it ring. Gen usually did too, but not this time. She jumped up off the floor and grabbed the phone almost as soon as it rang, like she was expecting it or something. I had never seen her move so fast. (She wasn't into sports.) At the time, I fig'red it was because she knew I was busy with hoe cakes, and she didn't want to wake Penny—that was our reasoning for doing most of what we did. *Don't wake Penny.*

I heard her mumble something in the other room before bringing the phone to me.

"It's High Alps," she whispered, holding her hand over the phone's microphone.

"What do they want?" I asked. High Alps never called me, and I wasn't s'pposed to be at work that day, so I had no idea what business they had with me.

Gen shifted her weight. She looked uncomfortable, like something was bugging her. "Here. Just talk to them."

"Hello?" I said, barely speaking into the phone. I wasn't really paying attention because the cakes were getting close to needing flipped.

"Rush, we're letting you go," my boss, Mac, said.

"W-What do you mean, sir?"

There's no way he's serious, I thought. I always showed up on time, even though I didn't have no car, and I never called off. Not once. I thought that it had to have been some sort of joke, but it wasn't.

"You didn't make sure that the loading zone was safe before closing down for the day. We can't have people breaking safety rules," he said.

There was only one time that I didn't make sure the loading docks were clear. It was a week or so ago, when Gen was standing next to me, telling me to hurry up because she was cold and we had a long walk back. Gen was the only one who knew that I didn't clear the zone, because I got to work early the next day and cleaned it up before anyone saw.

I set the phone down on the kitchen counter, completely forgetting about the hoe cakes. They sizzled in the oil, turning from golden to dark brown.

"Gen, I just got fired. For the loading zone thing."

"Really?" She sounded surprise, but she was always good at making her voice sound ways that she didn't mean.

"You were the only one who knew about that."

"What are you trying to say, Rush?" Her voice sounded angry.

"It must've been you who told on me!" Now my voice sounded angry, too.

"Why would I go and do that? They probably saw it on the security tape."

I felt bad for accusing her just then, because her answer made sense to me at the time. I believed her because I never would have thought she would do me dirty. But looking back, I don't ever remember seeing any security tapes up in the mountains. What use would High Alps have in filming the mountains, anyhow?

Gen was silent for a second, probably waiting for the appropriate amount of time to pass before she abandoned one touchy subject for another.

"So, does this mean we can go back to Oklahoma now?" she asked quietly.

I shot her a glare. "Cheese and rice, Gen! Just give it up."

"You said you wanted to stay for your job, and now you ain't got no job!" Gen fired back.

"It doesn't matter what I said. We're not leaving."

"It never matters what you say; you always go back on your word!" she cried.

I knew from experience that leaving the house was the only way to end a fight like that, so I told her that I was out of there, and I slammed the door behind me. She probably thought I was storming off in anger. I s'ppose that was half true. But really, I was heading down to Rex McNealy's to see if he had a job for me. I knew that he was looking for help at the hardware store a while back.

I checked my bank account on my phone as I walked: a measly nine dollars and eighty-five cents. I needed to find something fast so that I could put food on the table for Gen and Pens. It was my job to take care of them. I may not have been able to make Gen happy, but I wasn't going to let her go hungry.

Rex lived a few miles down the road from me and Gen. He was one of the richer folks in Silverheel, since he owned a couple of stores uptown. He could have been one of those mega milli'naires if he lived anywhere but Silverheel; I'm sure of it. He had the smarts of a good business owner. But I fig're he was like the rest of us who moved to that good-for-nothing town, just looking for a place to escape and willing to sacrifice everything else in our lives for it.

But for living in Silverheel, Rex didn't do too bad for himself. He didn't have to rent any of the old, drafty houses in the center of town like Gen and I did. He had his own A-frame, cedar cabin with floor-to-ceiling windows and plenty of acres to have fun on.

I met Rex's sheep, Ovis, before I ever met Rex. Ovis would look out of the cabin window as I walked by on my way to the trails. I didn't know that was Rex's sheep, or his cabin, until Rex brought Ovis down to the hardware store one day. I knew a lot about sheep from when we used to have a farm back in Fairhope, so Rex and I got to talking, and I was glad to call him a friend.

After a short walk, I was at Rex's door with my fingers crossed that he'd have a job for me. Everything was riding on Rex having an opening at the hardware store. I didn't have a plan B.

"Go on, git," I heard him yell at Ovis as he cracked the door open. Rex's face lit up. "Why, hey there, Rush! How are you doing?"

"Pretty good, sir. Can I come in?" I was relieved that he looked happy to see me.

"That's some weather, isn't it?" Rex asked as he led me inside.

I took a seat in front of his wood burner. He poured me a cup of hot water to warm my hands with, and I was mighty grateful for it. I cradled the cup, letting the steam warm my face. I was having a hard time finding the courage to ask him for a job.

"I, uh, got fired from High Alps," I started and then immediately wondered if I should've kept that detail to myself. "I was wondering if there was any chance you still needed help down at the store. You'd be doing me a real big favor."

Rex shook his head. "I'm sorry. I already filled that position."

I was real disappointed to hear that, but that seemed to be my luck those days. I thanked Rex and stood up to leave when he put his hand out.

"Well, wait a minute, Rush. I like you, boy, and I don't want to see you go without work. I know you have that pretty, little baby girl to take care of. I do have some trees that need taken down if you want."

"That'd be great, sir."

"When can you start?"

"Now's good for me, sir." And just like that, I was a logger like my pa. It was just a matter of time before I disappeared like him too.

It was an extra cold winter and more weather

was moving in. The wind whipped and bit at our skin as we hiked towards Rex's woods, and I was grateful that he gave me a pair of his snowshoes to wear. We stopped when we got to his barn, where Rex kept his milking sheep. He said that milking sheep were the only kind of animals worth having and that sheep's milk is the only milk we should be drinking. "More calcium and other vitamins," he said.

Rex's sheep were loud. They screamed and screamed like they were scared of something. The ones back in Oklahoma weren't half as loud.

"What's wrong with them?" I asked Rex.

"Oh, they're probably just hungry," he said, turning to the trees. "Right here's where I need the space cleared. We're going to add to this barn and get some more sheep. Start making sheep-milk soap and cheese, the whole nine yards. Think you can handle it?"

I assured Rex that I could, and he handed me an axe. I turned the wood handle in my hands, wondering what in the heck he wanted me to do with that. He seemed to read my mind:

"A chainsaw would disturb the sheep and spoil the whole batch of milk. Is that a problem?"

"No, sir," I lied, because I really needed the job. But in my mind, I was already counting the number of blisters I was going to have.

"Alright, I'll be back around supper time to come get you. Gertie's making pulled pork—you're welcome to stay."

I thanked Rex again and kept my head down to block the wind as I began chopping. The blade of the axe made small chips in the large tree trunk, and my palms were raw and throbbing before I fell a single tree.

Chopping is like digging—ain't nothing to keep your brain occupied, so my mind wandered. I started replaying the fight with Gen and muttering responses to myself.

You were the one who decided to move out here. No one made you do it.

And then I heard something that sounded like a cow, but I knew Rex didn't have no cows, on account of him preferring sheep. I turned around, thinking that one of the neighbors lost a steer or something. But this wasn't no steer. It was a gosh darn moose.

I had never seen a moose in real life before. If I had, I'd never have been in the woods alone; I'll tell you that much. That moose was as tall as the truck I used to have—about as long as it, too. I'd guess he weighed more than a thousand pounds. He was so big that I might've thought he was fake —something Rex planted there to scare other animals away from his sheep. But the moose's warm breath was making puffs against the cold air, so I knew he wasn't no decoy.

The moose didn't take his eyes off me. He knew about me, and I knew about him, so there was no sneaking away for either of us now. We were in this together, whether we liked it or not.

Pa taught me a lot about animals during our hunting trips, but there ain't no moose in Oklahoma. I knew Pa would know what to do, though, and I would have given anything to have him there.

The moose lowered his head and trotted in my direction. His tall, skinny legs looked wobbly under his oversized body. He stopped a few feet from me.

"What do I do, Pa?" I asked the winter air.

Look around, I imagined him instructing me. *Are there babies?*

I briefly took my eyes off the moose to check around me. "No babies."

Good. What's he doing?

I watched the moose put his ears flat against his head and smack his lips.

"I think he's warning me."

What do you do when an animal's warning you, son?

I fig'red I had three choices. I could play dead, like you do with the grizzles; I could back away slowly, like you do with the mountain lions; or I could scare him away like you do with the black bears.

I looked him over. He didn't have the large claws that grizzles do, or the razor-sharp teeth that mountain lions have. He was big, but he looked pretty harmless, like the black bears. Big, but skittish. I thought that he was probably just hungry and looking for food in the cold, lifeless winter like the rest of us. So, I thought the best way to deal with this moose was to call his bluff. I started yelling and waving my hands in the air.

"Go on, moose. Git!" I screamed at him.

I know better now.

Now I know that moose don't bluff.

The moose reared up, and I swung the axe at him, sinking the steel tip into the warm, soft flesh on his side. He let out a cry and brought his front legs to my chest, pushing me to the ground.

"Help!" I cried to no in particular. I was alone. Rex had gone back to his cabin and was well out of earshot. There was no one who could save me.

Protect your face, I heard my Pa say.

I curled up in a ball, with my hands over my head and my face buried in the snow. The moose lifted his hoof and slammed it against my body repeatedly, leaving bruises as big as my hand. Every inch of my body throbbed.

This is how I die, I thought. *The moose will crush my lungs, or I'll freeze to death, unable to drag myself back to Rex's cabin. It won't be long before the mountain lions come to tear the flesh from my body, piece by piece. And then the cy'otes will drag my carcass back to their den to share the leftover bits with their cubs. They'll pick my bones clean and scatter them throughout the woods. When Rex returns, there won't be any sign of me. Fresh snow will have fallen by that time, burying the tracks, and the blood, and the axe. I'm going to disappear into thin air.*

I regretted leaving Gen angry and not kissing

Penny goodbye. Gen would always remember me as the dead-beat boyfriend who tried to keep her from her family, and Penny, well, she wouldn't remember me at all. My obituary reappeared in my head:

Rush Kilmer. Born October 31, 1983, in Fairhope, Oklahoma. Disappeared in the Rockies, alone, on February 15, 2013. Presumed dead. Disappointed everyone. Missed by no one.

I was given a second chance, though, because I didn't die that day. Or maybe that was my third chance, given the time I almost died in the river. But either way, I was alive for the time being.

Everything was blurry when I woke up, but the pain was sharp. I was surrounded by white, beeping machines and curtains that hung from rails on the ceiling. I was in a hospital room. I never did trust no doctors, so I started pulling at the wires and tubes that tethered me to the machines.

Mama was the only one who ever took care of me. I s'ppose that I never really asked her, but I'm sure she didn't have no degree. She always knew how to fix me up right, though. If I had a scraped knee, she'd rub some of the goats' bag balm on it.

"The only wounds that bag balm can't treat are the holes of the heart," she would say as she rubbed the cloudy ointment on my skin. And she wasn't wrong. Those scrapes ain't there no more. They healed right up, so that's proof enough right there.

The doctors didn't have no bag balm. They had clear liquid in pouches that they fed me through my intravenous. It burned all the way up my arm.

My vision came back slowly, and I saw Gen standing across the room, next to the doctor. I recognized her right away. I could never forget her face. At first, I felt better knowing Gen was there; I knew I could trust her.

Rush! I expected her to say. *Thank God that you're alive! How could I have been so stupid as to let a little thing like where we live get between us?*

But none of those words came out of her mouth. She was staring at me like she didn't know me.

"Why are you looking at me like that?" I asked her.

"Rush?" Gen asked. She sounded more confused than concerned.

"Yeah?"

Gen turned her back to me and whispered something to the doctor. I didn't hear what they said, but when Gen turned around, her face twisted into a person that I ain't ever seen before; the town had finally changed her. Her wheels were turning.

CHAPTER 6

Oklahoma Knots

Gen left the hospital a little while after that, and I didn't see her for four whole days. That was the longest we'd been apart since she moved to Silverheel, if you can believe it. Before the moose attack, we spent every minute together. It was never enough, either. I can't think of a single time that we got sick of each other. Sure, we'd have small fights over things like moving back to Oklahoma, but they weren't no big deal. I still loved her to pieces, and I thought she loved me just the same.

I had a lot of time to think as I sat in the hospital by myself. The nurses would come in and fuss with my monitors all night, which meant I didn't get no sleep. So, I'd be awake at three in morning, thinking about Gen, and our relationship, and what she was doing instead of seeing me in the hospital.

And then I started to get pretty steamed at Gen. I mean, I knew she was mad at me, but wasn't she s'pposed to love me, after all? And ain't you s'pposed to visit the people you love when they're in the hospital, anyhow?

She never did apologize for that. I can't be surprised, though. In all the years that we had together, I don't think I ever heard her say sorry. Well, that's not true. One time, she did say, "I'm sorry you feel that way," which is more of a backhanded apology than anything.

But this time, when I asked her why she left me alone in the hospital, she just told me that she was busy taking care of Penny. I believed her at the time because that baby was a handful. We used to call her *Monster*.

Other people called her a monster, too, but on account of her eating all the time and putting on weight real fast. But Gen and I used to call her *Monster* because she had a hard time being happy. Even when you'd try to make her smile, she'd flash a big, gummy grin and then go right back to being mad because she wasn't going to let you win. I s'ppose that ran through Gen's blood, stronger than any white blood cells or oxygen or anything else in there, so I should've fig'red it was going to be in Pens too.

Penny would be seven now. Almost the same age that I was when I met Victor. Man, I miss that girl. I deserve it, I s'ppose. I did nothing but complain whenever she'd keep me and Gen up for nights on end, but I'd trade all the sleep in the world just to be able to see her again.

Gen showed up at the hospital once the doctors told her I could go home. I didn't know much about what was wrong with me or what kind of treatment I needed because they did all the talking to Gen. They said something about my head not being right enough to handle that information just then. I assumed they meant that the concussion made it hard for me to understand things. Looking back, I regret not asking questions and just letting Gen handle it all, but it didn't matter to me at the time—I was just glad to be getting out of that hospital and back home, where I could be with Gen and Penny.

Gen had a big ole smile on her face as she rolled a shiny, blue wheelchair into my hospital room. I was surprised that she was so happy to see me, given how we left things. In hindsight, her grin was the first thing that should've told me something was up. But at the time, I had come up with a perfectly reasonable explanation: I thought that she was happy because accidents change people; they make you start appreciating life and stuff. Surely, anyone in my shoes would've thought the same.

I told Gen that I ain't handicapped and that she should roll that wheelchair back to where it came from. But Gen said that the doctors wanted me to stay seated for now, on account of my head injuries.

Just as I 'spected, everyone stared at me (read: the wheelchair) as Gen rolled me through the hospital. And the whispers. Oh, the whispers. They didn't even try to hide it. They'd throw a loose hand over their mouth, but they didn't talk in no whisper. Pens was sitting on my lap, though, and she was a cute little girl, so I just fig'red that they were admiring her. I told myself that the meds were making me paranoid, but that was the second thing that should've clued me in.

There was a cab waiting outside the hospital to take me and Gen home. I thought for sure that was going to be the end of Gen's good mood. As soon as Gen saw that bright yellow paint, she'd think of Lumpy and she'd be sour again. But it didn't happen. She stayed happy. It was strangest thing I had ever seen. That was the third clue that I missed that morning.

Almost as soon as we got home, sometime around one, there was a knock on the door.

"Rush, this is Jasper—your nurse," Gen said as she let the stranger into our house.

"A nurse? I don't need no nurse." '*Specially no guy nurse*, I added under my breath. "How are we paying for this anyhow?"

"Insurance," Gen responded simply.

I was surprised right then, because we didn't have no insurance. We had a cheap plan with High Alps for a few dollars a check, but that was before Gen quit and I got fired. But I trusted Gen. I didn't have no reason not to. Plus, I knew she couldn't be affording no nurse out of pocket.

"It's nice to meet you, Rush." Jasper said with a smile. He was tall, much taller than me, with perfectly-styled, thick, dark hair.

I shook his hand, even though I had a mind not to, but I did it anyways because my mama raised me right.

Jasper looked to either side of him, expecting to find a coat rack or a side table like you'd see in some fancy foyer (or *foy-yay* if Gen was here to pronounce it in her smug, faux French accent). When he didn't find one, he frowned, folded his leather coat, and perched it on top of his medical bag.

"I'm going to go bathe Penny," Gen announced, out of nowhere.

"It's the middle of the day—," I tried to argue, but it was too late. She was already gone.

We always bathed Pens at night, right before bed, and I was afraid that bathing her right then would put her to sleep and then she wasn't going to sleep that night. That was all I ever worried about: Pens sleeping at night. Turns out, I should've been worried about more important things.

"Alright, let's get this IV in you," Jasper said as he led me to the couch. "It's morphine for your pain—it'll make you feel much better than any pill would. I promise."

That sounded like a heck of a deal to me, so I held my right arm out for him.

He fiddled with the syringe and then grabbed my elbow, right where I had a big, purple bruise. Pain shot through me. I yelled and tried to jerk away, but Jasper only tightened his grip. He mumbled an apology but he sure didn't look sorry.

"Okay, this will be a little uncomfortable," he said as he wrapped a rubber band around my arm and wiped a small, alcohol-soaked piece of cotton on my skin. Blood started to pool in my fingers.

Jasper had one of those, what Gen would call, heartthrob faces: a square jaw, dark brows, a strong-but-not-too-strong nose. Now, I didn't see it. I'm not saying he wasn't a good-looking fella, but not to the point where you'd go, *now he's a good-looking fella*. Gen thought so though. I could tell by the way she looked at him, like they had a secret between the two of them. I fig'red that was how I ended up with a boy nurse and not no girl nurse. It had to have been, because he sure didn't have those gentle, tender-loving hands that nurses should have.

Jasper slid the needle into my bulging vein and tacked a bag of clear liquid to the wall. It dripped slowly into my intravenous. He looked me over and gave me a slight smile, like he pitied me. I squinted back at him, because I didn't want no pity from no heartthrob nurse.

"Do you think we all have some bad in us?" Jasper broke the silence.

He had that godawful Cleveland accent with the thick, nasally *A*s, and he was using that fancy

Queen's English. I could tell he wasn't from around those parts, and I was already setting not to trust him.

"What do you mean?"

"I mean that we all have our secrets. For example, whenever I'm talking to someone, I focus on their worst feature—their ears, their nose, the little flab of fat that hangs from their chin, anything but their eyes. It makes people so self-conscious." He laughed.

I looked at Jasper for the first time since he started talking, and I realized that he was looking at my forehead. I stopped listening to him and started wondering if my forehead was too big. Gen never said so, and surely, she would've said something if it didn't fit my face. She was always real honest like that.

"What do you do that for?" I finally asked. I was getting the feeling that he messed with people's minds in other ways too.

Jasper shrugged. "Do you have any secrets, Rush?"

I shook my head, probably for a few seconds longer than I should have. *Doth protest too much*, I could hear Gen say in her sing-song voice.

"Oh, come on. You never lied to help anyone out? I mean, that type of lie could be understandable. I could probably think of, I don't know, twelve of my own."

I remember Jasper flashing his straight, white teeth, and then...nothing. The next memory I have is the smell of the Silverheel church. Gen used to drag me to that church every Christmas. I know I had no business being in a church but it made Gen happy. It probably made her feel a little less homesick on the holidays, I'd reckon.

The church had a distinct odor of old books and frankincense. "It's the smell of Catholicism," Gen would say. I thought that was what brought me back. I'd recognize that smell all day.

There were two deputies standing a few feet from where I was sitting on the church floor. One of them was fiddling with his camera while the other was talking on his cell phone, mindlessly flipping through a Bible.

"What's going on?" I asked as I stood up, realizing for the first time that I wasn't in the same jeans and t-shirt that I was wearing when I was at the house. I was in Gen's clothes. A dress, at that. I pulled at the bottom of the dress. It was long on her but it barely covered my important bits.

You pulled at the hem *of the dress*, is what Gen would say if she were here.

"Do we really have to go over this again?" The deputy with the camera asked. It was the same deputy that didn't do nothing when I called about Art. His name was Brian Hennessy, and he was just about the laziest person I had ever met.

"I'm sorry, sir. I'm not sure what you mean," I told him.

"Some poor woman walked in and found you tied up on the church floor. That's what's going on."

My stomach turned. I realized right then that I must've been drugged, and there was only one person who could've done it.

"It was Jasper!" I blurted.

Jasper was the last person I was with. He was the one giving me who-knows-what meds directly though my intravenous, where it hits you immediately. My skin crawled at the thought of what else Jasper could've done to me—what else he *did* do to me.

"Cut the crap, Rush. This right here is a self-tied knot," Brian said.

He handed me his camera. On it was a picture that I didn't remember anyone taking of me. I was sitting on the church's thin, magenta carpet, looking straight at the camera. My arms were wrapped in rope, and I was wearing Gen's plaid dress—the same dress that I had on right then.

I would've sworn it was a fake photo—something someone put together to mess with me. But my own arms told me the truth. They were red and chaffed from where rope had been just minutes earlier.

I concentrated as hard as I could, trying to picture Jasper tying me up, carrying me into the church, and leaving me for some unexpecting parishioner to find, but I couldn't remember a single thing.

One thing was certain, though. I didn't tie myself up.

"That's impossible," I told Brian.

Brian sighed and grabbed the rope off a pew. "I imagine any farm boy from Oklahoma would know how to tie a few different types of knots," he said as he formed loops around his wrists and stepped over his hands. He had tied his own hands behind his back, right before my eyes.

"But—" I started to say, but Brian cut me off.

"Look, Rush, if you admit that you did this for attention, I can let you go. I won't even charge you or anything like that, since this is your first offense. If you keep insisting it wasn't you, though, we'll have to keep you here on a seventy-two-hour hold and then see what a judge has to say about this mess that you've got yourself in."

Brian looked at the clock on the wall. It was five in the evening. I wondered if he was wanting to get home to dinner. I heard he got married a few weeks prior; no doubt that his new wife would have some hearty chili and cornbread waiting for him on the stove.

I knew what was in store for me if they put me on a seventy-two-hour hold. I'd be in a room with padded walls and bright lights—the kind of place that they put the crazies and the never-goods.

I had only been to that kind of place a few times before, when my mama took me to visit my Uncle Vernon. He wasn't right, they said.

He was a smart man—he could tinker with any 'lectronic and get it running again, even when my Aunt Millie would mess it up so badly that it wouldn't turn on. But that wasn't how most people in Fairhope knew him. They knew him for the wild stories he'd tell. Some days, he'd tell people that he went to one of those ivies up in Connecticut. And when they'd ask what his degree was in, he'd make up some story about getting expelled. Other days, he'd tell people that his name was Roy and that he owned three hundred acres of good, sweet corn in the next town over.

Everyone had their own ideas about why he made up those stories. My mama thought he was ashamed that he never amounted to anything more than a factory worker in Fairhope. Aunt Millie thought he really did believe what he was saying because other times, he'd be regular ole Uncle Vernon again. She said it was like there were two different people in there.

It was hard to see him change over the years when we'd go visit him. He was the same Vernon when he went in to that place, but each time I saw him, he lost a little bit of his smile until he didn't have one no more.

I sure didn't want to stay in that place for three more days, and I knew Brian wasn't going to believe me anyhow, so I told him what he wanted to hear.

"Glad to see you're cooperating, Rush." He took a few more pictures of my wrists and handed me a gray sweatsuit to wear home. For as useless as Brian was, I sure was glad he gave me the sweatsuit.

I limped home, on account of me not trusting to get in the car with strangers no more. The story made the news by the time I got back, around seven that night. Gen was sitting on the couch giving Penny a bottle. The news was on the TV.

"Rush, where were you? You left your phone here," Gen turned to me.

I opened my mouth to explain but the news reporter answered for me. We listened as she told me about my life, events that I didn't even remember.

"Rush Kilmer was found in woman's clothing in the Silverheel church today, with his arms bound. Police say that there are no signs of foul play and that he tied himself up. Deputy Brian Hennessy said, 'Residents don't need to worry for their safety. This man has admitted that this was a ploy to seek attention.'"

The reporter had a slight smile on her face. I bet she felt bad later on when she had to tell everyone that I vanished into thin air.

"I'm so embarrassed. I'm never leaving the house again." Gen put her head in her hands. There were only two thousand people or so in Silverheel, so everyone knew exactly who I was—who we were.

"You're embarrassed? How do you think I feel?"

I never thought I'd say this out loud, because I was s'pposed to be the man and all, but I was secretly hoping Gen would comfort me. At least, that's what I thought she was going to do. But she had already started on the interrogations, more of what I spent the last hour going over with the sheriff.

She peered at me, like she was determined to get a truth out of me, even if it wasn't the real truth.

"You got drunk, didn't you? And that's why you blacked out? You have been drinking a lot lately," Gen said before setting Penny in her bouncy seat and switching the TV to cartoons.

"I didn't drink no beer. It was Jasper! Where were you anyways? Why didn't you come looking for me?"

"You and Jasper were gone when I got done bathing Pens—I just fig'red you went somewhere."

"Where would we have gone, Gen?" I said, louder this time. Partly to talk over Penny's cartoons but partly because I was getting pretty fed up.

"What are you saying, Rush?"

"I'm—" I started to say before backing down. Fighting with Gen was the last thing that I wanted to do right then. "I'm not saying anything."

"Did you tell the sheriff about those pills you've been taking? Maybe you took one too many of those yesterday. Washed it down with the beer you say didn't drink." She eyed me from across the room.

She sure was making it hard not to fight with her.

"So, you don't believe me either?"

"I believe that you don't remember what happened. I'm just trying to be realistic. There's no way Jasper kidnapped you yesterday," Gen said, but with a softer voice this time.

Kidnapped. She made it sound so trivial, because grown men don't get *kidnapped*. And I know she did it on purpose.

Gen sat down next to me on the couch. She tried to run her fingers through my hair, but I smacked her hand away. By this point of the night, the cartoons had run their course, and Penny's whines turned from occasional to constant, which meant that it was time for bed and our fight would have to wait.

We went through the same motions that we did every night: Gen bathed Penny while I made a bottle and laid out her pajamas. Then, I fed Penny and rocked her to sleep. When we were done, Gen stayed up to watch TV, and I—not wanting to be in the same room as Gen—chose the bed.

I tried to sleep, but my mind was racing. I knew it was Jasper who drugged me. I just knew it. But why? What could Jasper want with me? And then it hit me: the heartthrob face, the not-so-tender hands. Jasper wasn't a nurse. He was a hitman. I couldn't believe I didn't see it sooner.

And then I remembered seeing someone who looked like Jasper when I was in the hospital. There was only a brief moment where he walked by my room, but it was long enough for me to notice his dark hair and his height.

So that was it. Jasper saw me in the hospital. He overheard the doctor tell Gen that I'd need a nurse, and he made himself available for the job. I was practically a sitting duck.

I'm a little ashamed to say that there was a list of people that would've wanted me dead. There was Kenny and Art, but that was four years prior, and I made it pretty clear to them that they better not ever come back to Silverheel.

That left one person. Ricky.

There was a time when Ricky helped me dig through the cafeteria garbage cans because I threw away my toy cars. We picked through all the leftover food that had mixed together, trying to keep our own lunches from coming back up, until he spotted the cars under someone's brown paper bag. And now here he was, paying someone to kill me so that I couldn't ever go back to Oklahoma.

And what a waste of his hard-earned money, I thought, considering how I wasn't even going back to Oklahoma no more. (Do you see my mistake? Did you catch on sooner than I did?) About five more minutes pass before I realized that I never did tell Ricky that I wasn't going back to Oklahoma.

That's it! I thought. All I had to do was text Ricky and then he'd call this whole thing off. I quickly typed a message on my phone:

Just forget I ever said anything.

I felt relieved as soon I said it. Ricky would say

"okay" and then I could finally rest easy and put this whole mess behind me. So, I waited. And I waited. But he didn't reply.

Just as I started to fall asleep, it was morning, and the crows were outside our window. Penny started to slam her legs against the crib mattress, which meant she heard them too.

"Darn crows," I muttered to Gen, but she just rolled over and ignored me. I guess that was her way of telling me that I better get up to take care of Penny.

Only twenty minutes or so had passed since I last checked my phone, but I held my breath anyways as I typed in the unlock code.

Still no text from Ricky.

That was night seven of next to no sleep. The first night was the night Lumpy died, the second night was the night I told Gen I changed my mind about going back to Oklahoma, and the four nights after that was when I was in the hospital. It was getting hard to remember things—my brain was mixing all my days up, but I'm pretty sure that Jasper showed up again midday.

I begged Gen not to open the door when I heard the knock, but she just said that there weren't any other nurse options in Silverheel and that we were lucky that Jasper could squeeze us into his busy schedule last minute. I wasn't in any shape to hold the door shut, as the bruises had turned a yellow and green shade by that point (not unlike the food in the cafeteria garbage can), so I did the next best thing. I checked for my insurance. It wasn't the kind of insurance that paid off Ricky's loan after I burnt up his truck, but it was the kind that was going to protect me if Jasper tried to pull something again. I ran my fingers along the underside of the couch cushion until I felt the smooth metal of my gun.

"Hey there, Rush. Nice to see you," Jasper said as he did the same coat-folding ritual as last time. His voice was loud and unvaried, like he was faking his cheerfulness.

"You're not sticking me with any needles," I told him flat out.

"He hasn't been sleeping well," Gen said to Jasper, apologizing for my attitude. She turned to me. "You look awful. Why don't you go back to sleep?"

It was an odd statement, considering how she could've gotten up with Penny if she thought I needed rest.

"I can't sleep," I told her.

Gen turned back to Jasper. "Do you have anything to give him so he could get some rest? And maybe we can skip today's visit?"

"I ain't taking any pills from him either."

Jasper dug through his bag and studied the label of a bottle. *At least he acts like a real nurse*, I thought.

"They're just regular, over-the-counter sleeping pills. You can check yourself," he said as he handed me the pills.

They looked real enough, and I was desperate

for sleep. I swallowed one dry.

"I'll get Penny out of the house so that it's nice and quiet for you," Gen said as she patted me on the shoulder.

I think I saw the Heavens part and the angels sing just then, because it seemed like Gen and I had finally turned a corner. And the snow wasn't even gone yet, to boot. We were so close to getting back to how things used to be. There was just one person left to deal with.

"Tell Ricky this whole thing's off. I'm not going back to Oklahoma anymore," I whispered to Jasper as soon as Gen had left the room.

Jasper looked puzzled. "What thing?"

"I know he hired you to kill me."

"Oh, boy. Maybe we should cut back on your meds. We'll figure all that out when I'm back tomorrow around twelve, okay?"

I don't know how much time passed after that. Could've been thirty minutes, could've been three hours. But the next thing I know, I'm waking up on my mattress. The sun was peeking through our living room window, so I knew it was daytime.

My head felt thick, and my arms were numb from the weight of my body. Jasper had tied me up and put me in one of Gen's dresses again. (If I had been able to see myself in a mirror, I would've noticed that he shaved my beard and put Gen's makeup on me as well, but I was going to find that part out later.) He was mocking me for what I did in Victor's basement.

The mattress squeaked as I shifted my weight off my arms. I froze and held my breath, listening for signs of Jasper. Eventually, I got enough courage to scream for Gen's help, for anyone's help, but it was no use. I was alone. It was a feeling I was getting a lot lately.

Sitting up was a chore, but I had finally managed. When I looked around the room, I saw what Jasper had done while I was drugged. All of the drawers and cabinets were hanging open—their contents were strewn around the room. I had no idea what he was looking for. We didn't have nothing worth anything. If we did, Gen would have lost it long ago.

And then a bright red color caught my eye. It was the color of blood when it's fresh and still ripe with oxygen. It was the same color that Gen would wear on her lips and her nails when we'd go out on a date, but this time, it was on the wall. My breath caught in my throat as I read.

NEXT TIME

This was it. Jasper was going to make good on what Ricky had paid him that money for. I was going to finally answer for my sins—for what happened in Victor's basement, for what happened to Ricky's truck, for leaving my mama, for keeping Gen from hers. And Jasper was going to be the one to help me answer for them.

I don't know how long I sat there, staring at those words. A long time, I'd guess. It was dark by the time Gen walked in and saw me.

"Gen, help!" I yelled as soon as I heard the jingle of keys in the door.

"Rush? What happened?" Gen dropped a grocery bag and ran over to untie me. A tub of vanilla yogurt splashed against the floor.

"Jasper drugged me again. I told you he was doing this to me!" I yelled as I dialed the sheriff.

Gen sighed. "Not that again, Rush. Jasper would have no reason for doing this. No one would."

Of all the deputies in Silverheel, it was Brian who showed up to our house. He strolled inside with one hand on his gun, and he treated me just the same as he did before. I can still see the look he gave me, like I was making this all up for attention.

"And what reason would Jasper have for drugging you and tying you up?" Brian raised an eyebrow at me.

I didn't have an answer for him. I knew Jasper had it out for me. I just couldn't tell Brian *why* because then I'd have to explain the part about Ricky's truck.

"Rush, I agree. This just doesn't make any sense," Gen butted in. She stood at the counter with the heel of her palms pressed against the butcher block.

"Gen—" I started.

"I'm taking Pens, and we're going to stay in a motel. You're not stable right now."

I knew Gen must've been fed up if she was willing to stay in a motel. There was only one motel in Silverheel, and it was only worth staying in if you got no other option. We had to stay at that motel one time when our apartment was being fumigated. We ordered pizza and drank beer. The pizza was for our bellies, but the beer was so that we didn't think about the motel room.

Gen grabbed Pen's diaper bag and walked out the door. I remember the last time we planned to go somewhere; we had to run around the house and make sure that we had everything—bottles, pacifiers, diapers, clothes, more clothes, wipes, bibs, the little thing that clips to the pacifier, formula, water for the formula, a blanket, diaper cream, eye flushing fluid, a booger sucker, and toys. And somewhere during all that, Penny would spit-up all over herself and need changed again. By the end of it, we wouldn't feel like going nowhere anymore. But this time, Gen grabbed the bag and walked out the door. It was already packed, like she was already planning on leaving.

CHAPTER 7

The Letter

Gen liked lists. She was always writing things down. They weren't normal lists though. Sure, she had the regular ole 'to-do' list, but she had some weird ones too, like a list of things she'd need if there was ever an apocalypse.

I told her one time, I said, "Gen, if there really was an apocalypse, you ain't going to have time to grab your list and start scratching things off it."

Gen just shrugged her shoulders and said that it helped her feel like she had things fig'red out. I knew her well enough to know that she just couldn't stand not being in control.

Most of Gen's lists were of no good to me, but I did begin to think that it'd be useful to have a list of the things that Jasper did to me. Not useful to me, of course, because I'd be dead.

But it'd be useful to other people—to Gen and Brian and everyone else who didn't believe me. Once Jasper finally did me in, they would want this list, for evidence and such. So, I counted the crimes, in no particular order:

Drugged me
Tied me up
Kidnapped me
Wrote threats on the wall
Dressed me in girl clothes
Dug through my stuff

I wasn't done fighting, but I knew my odds were no good. Jasper was a professional hitman, after all. Jasper was coming for me, and I was beginning to accept that he would probably kill me this time.

I wasn't scared, but I was sad. I was sad about all the things I would miss, like seeing Pens grow up. I was looking forward to giving her away at her wedding. And I would miss out on growing old with Gen. Boy, did I really mess it up with that girl. The pain was gone when I was with her, and I took her for granted. I got so comfortable that I forgot what it was like to not have her.

I didn't have no life insurance, so I wondered how Gen would get along without me. I worried about her being able to afford to take care of herself and Pens. But if I was being honest with myself, I knew it wouldn't be too long before she moved on and found someone else. She'd find someone to be the only pa that Pens ever really knew.

My mama taught me to always look on the bright side of things. "Find something good in everything," she would say, so I tried to distract myself by finding something good.

In my wallet was a picture that I took of my mama before I left Fairhope. I told her I wanted a picture because I was going to start taking more pictures. She didn't make me say it, but I'm sure she knew the real reason was because that would be the last picture I ever took of her.

I fig'red that I could be happy about seeing my mama again. I imagine that she was skin and bones by the time cancer took her the year before. "Riddled with cancer" was how Eli put it, and I was hoping that she would look like she did when we were younger. I'd say sorry to her for what I said that day I left Fairhope. I'd say sorry for leaving Fairhope to begin with. I hoped she'd forgive me.

"I'll see you real soon, Mama," I said to the glossy image.

I guess there's also the fact that people start caring about what you have to say after you're gone. No one ever did think much of me. Just a dumb Okie who never could make the right decisions to save his life; that's about it. But now I s'pect that you're hanging on my every word.

I could also be happy that if my death was anything like Jasper's games, I wouldn't be awake to feel any pain. My life would slip by me while I lie on the bathroom floor, or wherever he decided to do it. (I'd choose the tub, easier clean up that way.)

My future would disappear without me even knowing it. I s'ppose I should be grateful. Plenty of other people have it worse. Like my mama, who Eli said was in so much pain that she couldn't even eat. Or the wild goat that was screaming when Eli trapped and killed it when he was ten. No one should be screaming when they're dying. But they shouldn't die without knowing it either. I didn't want to lose something without even knowing that I was losing it.

So, I made up my mind to write Jasper a letter. I decided that it was the only way I could confront him, since he wasn't going to let me do it while I was of sound mind and body.

Dear Jasper, I started but then realized that sounded a little odd. *Dear?* Do you start a letter to your killer with *dear?* I scratched it out and tried again:

Jasper,

See you in Hell.

Rush

There, I thought. Cold and to the point.

I was never too good at sharing my feelings, but I thought I should write a letter to Gen and Pens, too, seeing how I wouldn't get to say my final goodbyes.

Dear Gen,

I love you more than you'll ever know. You were my world, and I hope you never felt like you were not. But I have a feeling that you did, and I'm sorry for that. I'm sorry that I never told you the truth. I was scared. I did some bad stuff in Oklahoma and I just couldn't go back. The law was going to get me if I ever returned. But if I could take it all back, I would. I would drive you and Pens to Oklahoma myself. And face up to what I've done. I missed out on all those years with my mama because I was running. I'm sorry that I almost made you do the same.

Goodbye, Gen.

Rush

I pulled out a new sheet and wrote one to Penny:

Dear Penny,

I want you to know that I've loved you from the moment I saw you on the picture machine at the doctors. The room was dim, and the radio was playing in the background. My favorite song was on—ask your mama to play it for you sometime. Your mama and I weren't sure if you were going to be healthy or not, but there you were. Your little heart was beating away. Then your mama and I found out that you were a girl, and I was so excited. I couldn't think of anything better than having a daughter. I already know you'll be as smart as your mama. And as beautiful too. I love you both with all my heart.

Everything I have,

Pa

I left the letters on the counter and sat down on the couch with a mason jar of crystal clear, corn whiskey 'shine. It was the finest you could find in the west. (No 'shine out west is truly good.) Rex brewed it whenever the weather was warm enough, and he gave me a jar that past Christmas.

"For something special," he said.

I thought I'd save it for when I turned thirty in October, but the very last day—the very last hour—of my life seemed like a special enough occasion. I twisted open the jar and took a big glug. It burned all the way down.

I sung softly to myself, swirling the liquid in the jar—the alcohol got smoother and my singing got worse with each sip. I welcomed the warm, fuzzy feeling that was beginning to grow inside my head.

And then the floor creaked.

"Gen?" I called out, or at least I tried to. It probably came out more like *Shen*, on account of the 'shine, but it didn't matter anyhow. The house wasn't big enough for her to sneak in without me noticing. If *Shen* had come home, I would've known.

I took more sips of the 'shine, until I could convince myself that the creaks were from the house settling, but the alcohol worked against me. My eyes became less reliable with each sip. Soon, I could see Jasper standing in the shadows with a long butcher knife in his hand, just waiting to drive it through my skull.

I kept sipping until my eyes became heavy enough that I no longer cared about Jasper standing in the shadows with his butcher knife.

"I see you, *Shasper*," I slurred at the empty corner. "You don't *shcare* me."

A few more sips, and I had finally drank myself to sleep. My hand fell open, spilling the rest of the 'shine on my lap.

A week of nearly no sleep meant that wet pants weren't enough to wake me. I didn't even want to wake up when I heard the angry pounding at the door. My fully-drunk, half-asleep brain was slow to rouse. But something told me I had to wake up, that my life depended on it.

"Gen?" I called out again (still not any more clearly), hoping that she had locked herself out. But her keys weren't on the counter. She didn't lock herself out. It wasn't Gen.

I reached for my insurance under the couch cushion, but my gun was gone. My heart raced. All the calmness that I had went right out the window. Turns out, I wasn't ready to die.

I crept towards the kitchen to grab a knife and then back to the front door, walking on every third floorboard to keep the floor from creaking. It was a pattern that I learned well from when Penny would be asleep.

The pounding turned into a violent jiggling of the door knob. The door began rattling on its hinges. This wasn't anything like how Jasper had gone about it before. Maybe he only had to be sneaky when Gen was around, I thought.

I reached for the handle, knife in hand, but the door gave way and flew open. The room was dark, but there was enough moonlight to see that the intruder wasn't tall, and he didn't have a heartthrob jaw or perfectly-styled hair.

He had a crooked nose and eyes that were just a tad far apart. He had Ricky's face.

"Ri—" I started to say, but Ricky wrapped his fingers around my throat and knocked me to the ground. The knife flew out of my hand and slid clear across the floor. I scratched at the wood, trying to get away from him.

Ricky tightened his grip around my neck. Breathing was getting harder. My vision narrowed. I could feel myself slipping away. My obituary appeared in my head for a final time:

Rush Kilmer. Born October 31, 1983, in Fairhope, Oklahoma. Murdered by his former best friend in Silverheel, Montana, on February 20, 2013. Disappointed everyone. Missed by no one.

Time of death? I imagined the coroner asking.

I squinted at the clock on the wall. "Twelve," I squeaked out with the little breath I had left in my lungs.

"Twelve?" Ricky repeated. I guess he had expected me to pick better last words.

And then I slipped away to the nothingness.

I didn't think it was God who saved me, given all the stories that I've already told you here, but I did believe I had some sort of charm. There was no other explanation for why my life would be spared not once, not twice, but three times.

But it's a well-known fact that, just like bad things, wishes only come in threes. The next time, I'd disappear for good.

I looked around the room. Ricky was gone. It was morning. The room was quiet. The knife was back in the block. The door was shut. It was like Ricky was never there. I walked over to the counter where my letters were still lying. There was a response underneath the one I wrote to Jasper.

It was in the same handwriting as the message on the wall—a peculiar use of all capital letters with the letter *E* so curved that it looked like a backwards three.

If Ricky wrote this letter, then that meant that he wrote on the wall too, which would've meant it wasn't just Jasper that had been doing these things to me. Ricky had been in Silverheel this whole time, watching, making sure that Jasper gave me my just desserts. My hands shook as I picked up the letter.

HEY RUSH!

THOSE LETTER YOU WROTE TO GEN AND PENNY ARE JUST SWEET AS PIE.

XOXO,

ELIZA

Now, I knew that Ricky was the one with all the smarts when it came to crimes and alibis, but I didn't see how this letter was s'pposed to make it seem like he was never there. Surely, the sheriff wouldn't believe it was some chick named Eliza who tried to strangle me to death. Right?

I crumpled the letter and threw it in the trash. If Gen came home and saw Eliza's name, she'd kill me. Maybe that's what Ricky was counting on?

I hadn't asked that question to anyone in particular. I hadn't even said it aloud. But I was answered just the same.

Hi Rush! I wrote the letter, a voice said.

It was a woman's voice. I thought maybe I really did die, and it was my mama, greeting me on the other side. But my mama's voice was deep and raspy. This voice was high-pitched and bubbly. I rubbed my head, convinced that I was hallucinating from a lack of oxygen. *I need more 'shine*, I thought to myself.

God says we shouldn't drink, she scolded me. *We must ask Him to grant us the serenity to accept the things we can't change. I'm Eliza, by the way*, the voice added. I could see her right then (as much as one can *see* someone in his head). She looked to be about my age, with blonde, curly hair that hung around fat cheeks.

Oh Lordy, I thought. *I'm hearing voices. I really do belong in the bin with Uncle Vernon.*

Don't take the Lord's name in vain, she told me.

"Don't tell me what to do," I snorted. It wasn't my finest comeback.

You're not very appreciative, seeing how I saved you from Ricky.

"What happened to Ricky?" I asked aloud, though it was clear that I didn't need to. She heard my thoughts; I couldn't escape her.

I got rid of him.

"Rid of Ricky?"

Yep! God will only bring you to it if he can get you through it. Just like when Jonetta made us start doing that...thing. I took over. I saved you.

I didn't know what *thing* she was talking about but that was probably for the better.

"So why are you in my head now?" I asked her.

You didn't need me after it stopped, so I went to the dark space. I've been there, waiting for you to need me again. But patience is a virtue, you know, and God rewarded me by letting me come back when the moose kicked us in the head.

"Okay, so if I just make peace with what happened in Victor's basement, then you'll leave," I said, truly believing that it would be that simple.

I closed my eyes and imagined that one of those

shrinks with thick glasses was swinging a pocket watch in front of me. It was then that I noticed Eliza's feelings for the first time. It felt...empty, like the sort of emptiness that you'd have if you spent your entire life waiting to be needed.

"I accept what happened. I'm fine now," I whispered in the quite room.

When I opened my eyes, my head was quiet. More quiet than it had been in a long time. I let out a deep breath, relieved to be free from—

Boo! Eliza appeared. *You can't just wish me away. You need me. Whenever you freak out, I take over.*

"I don't freak out." I rolled my eyes at her (at me? at us?).

Yes, you do. You can't handle when someone says twel—

"Stop. Don't say it. Wait—so you were the one tying me up the whole time, not Jasper?" I had finally put the pieces together. Gen was right; it may have been quicker if I started with the edge ones.

Tying us up, she corrected me.

"Fine. Us," I growled at her.

Well, yes, kind of—

"And you took my gun too?"

Yes, but—

That was the last straw. I needed to get rid of her. But first, I needed medicine for the stabbing pain in my head. The reflection in the bathroom mirror shifted quickly, from one of a man, aged twenty-nine, a person I knew as myself. To the girl with blonde curls, a girl I had never seen before that day, but I knew her just the same. I knew her thoughts.

I stormed out of the bathroom and slammed the door behind me, not that anyone was left behind to see. Because she was with me, always. I was no longer a person—I was part of a system, me and Eliza.

And then it dawned on me: I could use the dark magic stuff that Gen bought to cure the house from its coldness.

I'm not a demon, Eliza said. I felt bad for a moment there because I knew that I hurt her feelings. I could feel them like they were my own. But I pressed on, rummaging through our closet and grabbing everything that Gen and I used the last time—candles, sage, pages of chants. I tried everything, but nothing worked. She was still there every time.

I stumbled over to the couch and put my head in my hands. A jitteriness started to build inside me. I felt uncomfortable, uneasy. *Why do I feel like this?* I wondered.

I need to pray, Eliza answered. *Can I take over for a little while, please?*

I didn't care one bit about Eliza's feelings, but I hated feeling so jittery, so I told her that I'd just do the praying for her.

"Our Father, who—" I started.

It's not the same. Please, she interrupted.

Then I remembered the other thing that Gen

used to say about the ghosts. She said they had too much leftover business and that's why they couldn't crossover. I fig'red that this was why Eliza was hanging around. If she could just pray real good one last time, then she would go away. Her soul would move on.

So, I agreed to let her take over. The transition only took a matter of seconds, but it felt like minutes. First, it started in my hands. I could no longer feel my hair between my fingers. Then, I lost the feeling of my elbows on my thighs and the couch underneath me. I could no longer feel the stabbing headache that I had just a second ago. I couldn't feel anything.

Eliza stood up from the couch, but instead of kneeling on the ground to say her prayers, she headed straight for the closet—the one where we kept our luggage. She skipped over my black suitcase and reached for Gen's light purple one.

It was lavender, Gen would say if she were here.

Hey! What's going on? I demanded to know as Eliza started shoving Gen's clothes into her suitcase.

"You had the last twenty-nine years; I get the next twenty-nine," Eliza snipped.

Oh, heck no, I thought. I was going to be trapped in that body forever. *Eliza, you give me control right now!* I screamed at her.

Just then, Gen walked through the door with Penny and the diaper bag that she took the day before. And I thought for a second that I was saved. I thought, there was no way Gen would let this girl just take over my body and walk out the door.

"Hey there, pretty lady!" Eliza smiled at Gen.

You two know each other? I asked them, but Eliza didn't answer me, and Gen couldn't hear me.

"Eliza?" Gen looked about as surprised as I was. "What are you doing here?"

"Ricky showed up last night," Eliza started to explain as she held up a pair of Gen's jeans, trying to fig're out if they'd fit her.

"He what? So how did you get control?"

"Rush let—"

"Wait, Rush knows about you?"

YES! I wanted to scream. Eliza said it for me.

"So, he can hear me right now?"

YES! I screamed again.

Gen's face fell. "Can I say goodbye, please? I promise to bring you back."

I could feel Eliza's reluctance. Now that she had a few tastes of the light, she didn't want to give it up, but she did as Gen asked. I began to feel the weight of my body again. I found myself in the bedroom, standing face-to-face with Gen.

"What in the heck is going on?" I asked her the moment I could feel my lips and tongue.

"I'm going to Oklahoma, Rush. And I'm taking Penny."

"Oh, no you ain't," I growled, trying to fig're out how to get Penny from Gen's arms without hurting her.

"Do you remember the two guys in the lodge

that day Lumpy died?"

"What's your point, Gen?"

Gen carried on, ignoring me. In true Gen fashion, it took her a while to get to the point. She wanted to explain every detail. I'll admit that, in the past, I would've just tuned her out at that point. Her stories often got to be too long and off-track. This story, though—this story was one that I listened to each and every word that she said. I will transcribe it for you now in as much detail as I can manage:

Mr. Construction and Hemorrhoids were standing outside the lodge when Gen went to take the trash out.

"Hey hon," Hemorrhoids called out to her.

She turned toward him, ready to go off on him (again), but she could see that he was trying to apologize.

"I'm sorry about earlier," he said. "We had a little too much champagne with our orange juice this morning, I guess."

Gen shrugged her shoulders. (The men probably saw this as Gen blowing them off, but you're asking for too much if you think Gen's going to say, "Okay, I forgive you.")

"So, I'm guessing you're not born and raised in Silverheel?"

"Fairhope. It's in Ok—"

"Yeah, I know Fairhope. Rush Kilmer used to live there."

"How do you know Rush?" Gen asked, suddenly

interested in the conversation.

Hemorrhoids paused, like he was fig'ring out how much to give away. "We were almost business partners once. He chickened out, though, and wanted his money back. It's a shame; he could've made a lot of money. He could've been able to leave Silverheel like I did. I only come here to vacation now."

"Rush never would've left Silverheel anyways," Gen mumbled as she launched a trash bag into the dumpster. "I want to go back to Oklahoma, but he won't let me take our daughter."

The man dug through his pocket and pulled out a business card. "You have more choices than you think you do when you live in a town like Silverheel, darling. Here's my number. Give me a call if you want some help getting back to Oklahoma."

Gen looked down at the card. At the very top was a name that she had heard before: Art McCraw. She shoved the card in her pocket without any real intention to call him. She remembered the story I told her about how slimy Art was, and she was rightfully skeptical of his offer to help. Was it really because he felt guilty about what he said to her that morning? Or was it to get back at me?

Of course, you already know what happened after that: I told her we were going, and then I told her we weren't going. Well, after I gave her the excuse about not wanting to leave because of my job, that sneak of a Gen called my boss while I was in the shower and told them all about the safety rule that I broke.

She was so mad at me that she had half a mind not to go see me when Rex called to tell her that I was in the hospital, but she went to see me anyways. And boy, was she glad she did.

"Looks like the moose got you good," Gen said as she walked into the hospital room.

(This is where I called her out on those being her first words to me in the hospital, but again, she just ignored me and continued with the story.)

"Hi Gen! It's me, Eliza. The moose sure did get us good," were the words that came out of my mouth.

Gen thought I was messing with her, but then Eliza told her all the secrets that I tried so hard to keep from her. And Gen knew me well enough to know those weren't the kinds of things I'd ever tell her.

And then Gen got an idea in her head.

"So, tell me, Eliza. Do you like being stuck in the dark while Rush gets to have all the fun?" Gen asked as she poured some ice water into a plastic cup.

Eliza said she did not.

"Hmm. I see." Gen pretended to consider the possibilities. "I hate to think of you stuck inside there. If only there was some way that we could help you take control."

"There is," Eliza said eagerly, "but Rush is too strong. I'll take over for him whenever someone says *twelve*, but Rush won't let me stay in the light forever. He'll push forward. I can feel him trying to come back now."

"Rush has always been hardheaded." Gen swiped her foot against the speckled linoleum floor. "So, maybe we'll just have to fig're out how to make him weak enough so that he can't push through."

And the best way to break a man's spirit? Make him think he's going crazy.

So, the two of them hatched a plan. Eliza would go away and keep coming back until I lost my mind.

The problem with that was I would never be scared of Gen, what with her being short enough to pass for a large child. Gen needed outside help. She needed someone for me to be afraid of.

"I could use your help if you're still offering it," Gen said when she called up Art.

She was smart enough to keep most of the details to herself. Gen told Art that she needed someone to say a certain word around me because I had a phobia that she was trying to help me get rid of. She explained that the person had to be undercover because I'd never agree to it.

Now, of course, I would've recognized Art any day of the week, so he got his friend to do it—the other guy in the lodge that day.

Mr. Construction, or Jasper, as I knew him, lived in a million-dollar home in Bar Harbor, Maine—the same town as Art. He was also concerned about karma, apparently, and he agreed to help

Gen out because of the way they treated her that day Lumpy died. It was Art's idea for Jasper to pose as my nurse.

Gen paid off the doctor so that he wouldn't tell me nothing about my condition. But I have reason to s'pect that he told the whole rest of the hospital. No one ever saw someone like me in a small town like Silverheel, and the nurses were gossips, probably whispering to each other over vials of fresh blood.

Over the next four days, Gen planned and prepared. Jasper flew in from Maine, and Gen told Eliza to pretend to be me whenever he was around.

After Jasper came to the house and hooked up the IV (which was a simple solution of water and salt, I learned), he brought Eliza back with the code word as Gen had instructed him to.

He was a polite man, so he did what he was asked and left without any further disruption. Eliza didn't say goodbye to him, because she was s'pposed to be me after all, and I wasn't keen on Jasper.

"Ready to go to the church?" Gen asked Eliza once Jasper left.

Eliza slipped the IV out of her arm and looked down at the orange t-shirt and jeans that she had on. "Can I change first?"

Out of habit, Gen led Eliza to my side of the closet, but Eliza wasn't interested in graphic tees. Her eyes lit up when she saw Gen's plaid dress. Gen said she had to try hard not to laugh when Eliza squeezed into that outfit.

The rest of the day was methodical and planned, like the night I burnt up Ricky's truck: Gen and Eliza secured some rope from the shed out back and walked to the church, where Gen tied Eliza up. Eliza let me come back once the sheriff was there. Gen knew that someone would find me and that the sheriff wouldn't care. They didn't want to do the paperwork.

The next day started out just the same. Eliza took longer in Gen's closet on this day, mulling over the choices (they were limited, given the size difference between me and Gen). Eliza selected one of Gen's summer dresses and admired herself in the mirror before helping herself to Gen's makeup bag.

Eliza was as useless with a mascara tube as I would've been, and Gen took pity on her. Gen instructed Eliza to take a seat on the couch while she went to grab a wet washcloth.

As Gen wiped Eliza's face, she started to frown.

"What's wrong?" Eliza asked.

"I don't want to cause problems or nothing, but since you're so into Jesus and all, I thought that maybe you'd like to know that you're sitting. . ." Gen trailed off. "No, never mind."

"What? Sitting on what?" Eliza had taken Gen's bait.

"Sitting on a gun," Gen clarified.

Eliza shot straight up, like someone had lit

the couch on fire. She reached under the cushion, grabbed the gun, and tossed it in the trash. Then, she tore through the house, looking for more contraband as Gen packed the diaper bag.

"Hey, I have an idea," Gen said as she picked up a lipstick tube. "We should write on the wall to scare Rush. That'll teach him for having a gun."

Eliza thought that was a neat idea. They took some time to come up with what to write, and when they were done, Gen helped Eliza tie her hands again.

Gen told me the plan was for Jasper to mess with me for a few more weeks. They had cooked up quite an elaborate scheme, but Ricky showed up that night and cut everything short.

"Just completely ruined everything," was how Gen put it.

"How could you do this to me?" I asked Gen when she was done with her story.

She switched Penny to her other hip as that baby was nearly eighteen pounds by that point. "You always told me that there ain't no laws in Silverheel—that your actions are between you and God only, because the sheriff ain't going to come after you. Well, I know that God will forgive me. I did what I had to."

"Please, Gen. Give me a second chance. I'll do anything. We can go back to Oklahoma," I begged.

"But this wouldn't be the second chance. Would it, Rush? I think this would be number..."

"Gen, no!" I knew what she was about to say.

"Number...twelve."

It happened faster than the last time. I was floating inside my body again; my voice was trapped in a dark skull. Eliza was in charge—my body wasn't mine no more.

"You should hear the things Rush is thinking about you right now," Eliza told her.

"I'd rather hear what you think about leaving tonight for Alabama." Gen phrased it like it was optional, but it wasn't no option.

"Sounds perfect!" Eliza shoved more of Gen's things into the suitcase.

"Not that one." Gen grabbed a necklace out of the suitcase and held it to her chest. A gift that I had given to her on our first anniversary. I guess Gen did have a sentimental side after all.

Gen made Eliza promise that she'll never leave the religious commune that she was headed for, and then Gen got herself a little of her own insurance to make sure I'd never be in control again.

"You know, Eliza," Gen said as she walked to the kitchen and returned with a knife, "we never finished our plan since Ricky showed up, and I'm worried that Rush ain't weak enough. There's only one way to make sure you'll never lose control."

I watched helplessly as Gen motioned for Eliza's arm. Obedient as she was, Eliza held it out and stood as still as possible while Gen carved a tiny '12' into her skin. I couldn't feel the pain because I was on the inside, but Eliza sure screamed a lot. The carving was small enough that it would pass unnoticed, a cat scratch, someone might think from a distance, but it was there nonetheless. And it was going to keep me trapped inside this darn body forever.

Gen dabbed the blood with a towel before giving Eliza a hug. The two had a heart-to-heart of sorts. From what I gathered, they started to get close over the last week. I guess what they say is true about bonding over mutual enemies.

But no amount of bond could keep Gen from Oklahoma or Eliza from the religious commune, so the two of them said their goodbyes and walked out the door.

That was the last day I saw Gen and Pens. Eliza told me that we were going someplace where we could get right with the Lord for what happened in Victor's basement, and I didn't have no say in it.

The drive to the commune was long and tiring, so Eliza pulled into a motel one night. We ended up staying there for a week or so; I think Eliza saw how fun the world could be and started to doubt whether the commune was even somewhere she wanted to go. But then we saw Eli on the news, pleading for my return. He said that he noticed Gen around town and that it didn't take him long to fig're out I was missing. Eliza knew that our face being on the TV was no good for her or Gen, so she jumped in the car and drove the rest of the way to the commune.

I'm guessing Eli tried reaching the sheriff in Silverheel, but I'm sure they never returned his calls.

All of Eli's efforts were for nothing. I'm not ever getting out of this commune. I knew that from the moment I met the man in charge, Father Josiah.

When Eliza first got there, Father Josiah asked her if she had a car or any money because all of your property becomes the Community's. Eliza gave him the only five dollars that she had. Father Josiah frowned at the small bill and said that since she can't contribute financially, she'll need to work in order to earn her keep.

Meals consist of chunky brown slop that they refer to as 'stroganoff,' poured onto plastic trays by members that have been designated as the servers. Every drop must be eaten, as wasting is a sin. The men eat first. Women eat last. I'm not sure why; Father Josiah doesn't like when anyone asks a lot of questions.

Everyone here wears a navy-blue uniform with fabric shoes. The showers are locked, except for six to six-thirty in the morning, and there are no outside communications allowed. Televisions, cell phones, and newspapers are all forbidden.

I've only seen one person try to leave: a man by the name of George Redox. Father Josiah beat on him in front of the entire Community for reading a biology book. He tried to escape that night. He was nearly out the front door when he came by a young boy with a red circle sewn into his shirt. The boy lifted a whistle to his mouth, and Father Josiah appeared just moments later. I haven't seen George since.

I told Eliza that we had to get out of there, but she just pushed me to a darker place. Now, I can't even see what's happening.

I haven't seen the sunlight since that day. I spend my days in the darkness; I imagine this is how it would be if someone was paralyzed and unable to speak, see, or hear, but their brain kept turning.

All I have to keep me company are my own thoughts. Thoughts of life before I went missing. Thoughts of what life might be like now. My only hope is that someone will be able to bring me back someday. But for now, all I can do is wait.

CHAPTER 8

My Story

I'm never alone, even when I think I am. Even when Penny is playing in the other room, and the house is quiet except for the sound of rain on the roof and the soft piano ballad that's coming from the stereo. Even when I think that I might be able to relax and that I could do something as simple as grab a can of tomato soup from the pantry —just like that, Rush is there, uninvited, unwelcome.

Goddammit, Rush. I swear at him, loudly, but he doesn't care. He never leaves me, not really. He follows me, waiting in the dark corners until he finds his way back in: into the kitchen, into the bedroom, into the shower—wherever I happen to be, he's there too, as real as he ever was. I never know when he will show up. It's been seven years, and I'm no better at avoiding him now than I've ever been.

They say that if you really want to know someone, then travel with them.

But that ain't true; is it, Rush?

We drove across the country together on our way to that concert in 2005, crammed in that tiny rental for God's sake. Surely, that would be enough to truly know someone if it were possible.

And we passed every test; didn't we, Rush? I asked aloud but he didn't answer. He never does.

We didn't get sick of each other when we were tired of listening to the radio or counting license plates, and the only thing left to do was to talk. We didn't fight when I was s'pposed to give you directions but I couldn't read the map, and we drove in circles until we finally stumbled on the hotel in Rapid City. We didn't disagree on which route to take—the shorter one, of course, even though we were more likely to hit snow. But even after five states and fourteen hundred miles, I still didn't know the real you.

Who is the real Rush? I don't think he knew. But the Rush that he sold me—the one that he convinced me to believe in—that's the one that always comes back to me. And I hate it. I want the other Rush, the one that I didn't know until it was too late. I wish it was Other Rush in the kitchen with me, because he's the one that's so easy to hate.

But I never get Other Rush. I get the nice one. The memories invite themselves in, like unwanted guests at parties. They show up, unannounced, and then they leave me, standing there like an idiot, with whatever mess they made.

So, there I am. Nice Rush is with me, and I'm standing in my kitchen with a can of tomato soup. And then we're not in my kitchen anymore. We're walking down the middle aisles of A & B, Silverheel's only grocery store. I'm trailing behind him, adding up our grocery bill as he tosses items in the cart.

"How much for tomato soup?" I ask.

"Two dollars and fifty cents," he replies.

That was how our conversation went each time he would grab something new, and then I'd tell him how much we spent so far. I had the very important job of making sure that we didn't go over fifty dollars or however much we had in our bank account that day.

No matter how hard I try to forget Rush, to forget grocery shopping, I feel trapped, destined to wander the aisles with him forever.

I force myself to leave Rush in A & B, and I'm suddenly aware that my throat's on fire. I bring my hands to my neck to check—no, no fire. Just heartburn. I felt the same kind of burn when I met Rush. But it was a good burn then, a burn I had mistaken for love. There was no love left anymore, just a sickening acid.

I put the tomato soup back and wandered across the kitchen, looking for something to sooth my throat. I tapped the screen on my fridge, and the glass lit up to reveal single-serve tubs of lime Greek yogurt, neatly stacked on the shelf.

How much did this yogurt cost? I wondered. I couldn't even remember the last time I had to pay attention to grocery bills. Five dollars? More? That's when I realized I didn't even buy the yogurt myself. Margot, my assistant, did the shopping for me most times.

Penny padded into the kitchen as I dipped my spoon into the bright green yogurt.

"Can I have some?" she asked. Her eyes were big and round.

"Sure, baby." I brought the spoon to Penny's tiny lips. She started breathing heavily, a sort of hyperventilating that she's done at the sight of food ever since she was a baby. She parted her lips eagerly, but her face quickly scrunched and her head pulled back in a recoil from the tart lime. She had a distinct look of bewilderment on her face, or maybe it was a look of betrayal. Perhaps both.

I brought the spoon back to her mouth, but she refused. She pressed her lips together and ran back to her room—she wouldn't be fooled again. Maybe she is my child after all, I thought.

I sat back down on my tan, leather sectional, in the same pair of white sweats that I had been lounging around in all day. A much-welcomed breeze floated through the window, carrying the smell of honeysuckle and rain. I closed my eyes and breathed in the fresh scent—honeysuckle quickly became my favorite thing after moving to Edgewood, South Carolina, two years ago.

It's not that there was anything wrong with Fairhope—believe me, I wasn't trying to run away from nothing like Rush always was. Fairhope just ain't the kind of place you live once you have money.

I thought about moving to New York City at first. That's where people who have money go, after all. I imagined living in a skyrise, with windows instead of walls. My apartment would be clean and modern. I would finally fig're out all the boroughs—is Manhattan the same as the Upper East Side, or are they different? How do you pronounce *haute* anyways? But then there's the other side of New York—the winter side, where people are dodging brown slush on the sidewalk and prying their wipers from frozen windshields.

We got a few inches of snow in Fairhope each year, but New York City gets twenty-five, and Silverheel: one hundred and five. No. Thank. You.

Rush used to say that snow in the mountains was important, because without enough snow, there wouldn't be enough run-off when it melts, and wildfires would spread. But that didn't make me hate the snow any less.

Rush doesn't know it, but he was the reason why I chose South Carolina. He wanted to live on the highest point of the mountain—up in the clouds, where he could pretend like real life ain't real. So, I chose the Lowcountry; with ground so low that it dips into the saltwater marshes that surround it. It's ground that'll remind you how close you are to sinking—to losing it all—with one wrong step.

That was the difference between Rush and me, though. Rush wasn't a fighter. He just kept running. And I just wasn't made like that. So now you see why I did what I did. Rush didn't leave me no choice.

I bought my home the day it went on the market. It's as gorgeous as you can imagine: an eighteenth-century colonial with huge, white pillars and a brick porch. The driveway is lined with oaks that are dripping with Spanish moss, and the willow trees are as tall as the house. Rush always hated those willers. He said they create too much of a mess, but I don't know nothing about that, because I just pay someone to clean them up.

My mama said the house was too extravagant when I bought it.

"What in good heavens are you going to do with forty-nine hundred acres?" she asked me. I could see her doing the math in her head, at three thousand dollars an acre.

"I got it all fig'red out, Mama," I said. And I packed her and my pa up and moved them to South Carolina. I got my pa some help down here, and he's doing better now. He hasn't had a drink in a year, and Mama and I are so proud of him.

I was worried about moving here at first; there's a lot of old money in the Lowcountry, and mine was new, to say the least. There's quite a few of them milli'naire heirs and heiresses—with money that has been passed down for hundreds of years, only growing with each century. It was something my mama and pa couldn't give me, but it's what I plan to give to Penny. She'll be an heiress to my fortune; that's one thing that Rush did for her, at least.

I'm set to marry one of those heirs early next month, but I s'ppose that anyone who has the internet already knows that. Not many people know the story of how we met, though.

It was mid-April, and I had only been in Edgewood for two weeks or so when I received an invitation to brunch in the mail. I wasn't sure how or why I got that invitation, as I hadn't met a single person in that town yet, besides my real estate agent. (I have since received similar invitations, so I now s'pect that once you become someone, you get added to a 'list.') I guess they were kind enough to look past my new money on account of my fame.

The morning of the brunch, I put on a peach-colored dress that I had bought just for the event and will probably never wear again. I left Penny with my mama and showed up to the brunch alone.

When I was poor, I thought that brunch was breakfast that you ate at ten o'clock instead of eight. I was wrong.

First, brunch is not a meal but an occasion. Bagels with lox and cream cheese, eaten leisurely between sips of mimosas because you have nowhere to be on a Tuesday morning, is brunch. A granola bar that you grab on your way out the door, to eat while you sit in rush hour traffic at six-thirty in the morning, is breakfast. Second, you don't find fiancés at breakfast. You find them at brunch.

This brunch was held in a grand hall in downtown Edgewood. Once there, I made a beeline for the buffet and piled my plate high using the strategy that Rush had taught me: focus on the things that cost the most, like the smoked meats and fancy cheeses with the wax still on them. As I reached for the brie and bacon quiche, I locked eyes with a man who was standing on the other side of the buffet table. He was gorgeous, with blue eyes and golden-brown hair. He was holding a small plate—more of a saucer, maybe—that had tiny bits of food on it, mostly fruit and pieces of pastry.

He looked down at my plate. It was twice as big with five times as much food as his.

"Hungry?" he asked.

"As a matter of fact, I am," I said with a head toss.

I had to admit that he was right. The small mountain of food was probably enough for the first trip to the buffet, so I turned to find a table, but not before grabbing several pieces of avocado toast.

I had never eaten at a table with place settings that had more than one fork, but somewhere along the way, I did learn that you start on the inside and work your way out. So, I took a seat and reached for my inside fork. As I bring a bite of quiche to my mouth, the man from the buffet line takes a seat next to me. I looked around the room at all the other empty seats and then back at him. He pointed to the silver, laser-engraved place card in front of him and raised his eyebrows in a sort of "so there" way.

"I'm Carter," he said (which did, in fact, match the *Carter W.* on the place card).

"Hello." I gave him my first name, but not my last. People don't recognize my face, but they recognize my name, and I wanted to keep that to myself.

We picked at our food in silence, and a few more people joined us. Their plates looked like Carter's. I looked around the room—everyone's plates look liked his.

One of the men at our table, who looked to be about my age, noticed that I was wasn't one of the regulars.

"Is this your date, Carter?" he asked, while looking at me.

I paid careful attention to Carter in that moment, hoping that he'd shake his head in a light, slightly regretful "nope," instead of a "hard-pass, no way" sort of way. After much analysis, I'd like to think it was the regretful kind.

"So, what do your parents do?" the man asked

me.

"Trent. Stop," Carter hissed.

"It was a simple question," Trent said with a slight smile.

I had no idea what was happening, but Carter knew. He later told me that Trent was looking to find out whether I was one of them or not. Acceptable answers were hedge fund manager and lawyer. Of course, my parents did neither. I told the table that my mama was in domestic work back in Oklahoma.

"Your mother was a maid?" Trent laughed.

"That's enough, Trent," Carter said loudly—loud enough that the entire room put down their inside forks.

"Do you have a problem, Carter?" Trent stood up.

"Yeah, I do." Carter stood up too.

"Boys!" one of the women at the table said through gritted teeth. She motioned for them to sit. She was wearing an elegant pant suit, and her graying hair was pulled back in a tight bun. Pearls hung around her neck and on her ears.

As it turns out, the elegant woman was Carter's mama, and sitting next to her was his pa. Carter's behavior mortified them. They shot him a glare.

The thing about mortification is that it bounces back to you, so it bounced off his mama and pa and right back to him. Carter sank in his seat and drained his champagne flute.

"Thirsty?" I asked.

"Did you not see the show just now?"

"Oh, I did," I smirked as I took a sip of my sunrise mimosa. "I'm surprised you haven't snuck out the back door by now."

"I don't run away from my mistakes," he said.

I put down my glass and turned to him. "You know, I like you more by the second."

And that was how Carter and I met, and how I knew he was nothing like Rush.

Perhaps it's clear by now, but Carter ain't the kind of man that you'd think of when you think of old money. He ain't dapper (his hair and clothes are always a mess—it drives his mama mad), and he certainly ain't suave. Sometimes, he acts more new money than I do.

I can't say that Carter and I never fight. We fight about the kinds of things that old money and new money would fight about. I still think that macaroni and cheese is dinner, and I refuse to try caviar. Carter insists that milli'naires don't find meals in small, cardboard boxes, but I don't pay him no mind.

Right before I left Fairhope, I went to that dairy stand one last time. I ordered a peanut butter cone and watched that same dairy lady make a mess of that swirl, but I didn't say nothing this time. There was nothing to say, really. Rush taught me a lot of lessons without ever knowing he was teaching me. I had to learn most of them the hard way, and one of those lessons was that you can't ever change someone who don't plan on changing.

I don't miss Fairhope much, and I try not to miss Rush. I try to miss things that matter, like the leaves on the willers when the storm blows them over. It wasn't always that way, though. I spent a lot of time thinking about what kind of person Rush was and wondering whether I had misjudged him, or whether I had misjudged me.

I was ten the first time I ever wondered if I was a good person or a bad person. I envied the people who never had to ask that about themselves. Like my mama, who's just a good person and no one ever questions it.

Every Sunday, I would watch as the gold bowl was passed around the church. You could always tell who didn't really have the money to contribute. They'd wait until the very last moment to dig for their wallet and then pull out a few bills under the pressure of everyone else's eyes. Not my mama, though. Mama was like the poor widow in the Bible who gave all the money that she had left. My mama wasn't a widow. We had Pa, but he spent his days drinking, so it was just the same.

Mama didn't have any more money than the rest of the parish, but she was always ready to put some in the collection plate. I watched my mama put her last three dollars in that plate every week. The priest said that made her a good Catholic.

The gold bowl would make its way back to the priest, and he would always set it on the table before stepping off the chancel to say goodbye to everyone. It would have been so easy to sneak back there and steal the bowl. I imagined how many cookies and snack cakes I would buy at the Fairhope Country Store—the ones Mama always said she didn't have no money for, right before Pa would grab a fistful of bills from the glass jar and leave to go buy smokes and booze.

But I never stole the collection plate money. My mama said that it was for the people who had even less than we did. We had a roof and cornbread, she told me as we walked home from church one day. I could feel the concrete through the soles of my shoes, so it didn't seem that way. But she said some people don't even have that.

Then, when I was eleven, there was a spider on my quilt. I didn't know what to do, so I asked my mama if I should kill it. She said yes, without even hesitating. I was surprised that a sweet person like my mama could be so uncaring towards an innocent spider, but if my mama said to do it then it must be right, I thought. So, I killed it. I didn't feel guilty about it either, because my mama said it was either him or me. I s'ppose that's why I don't feel guilty for doing what I did to Rush.

On the drive back from Silverheel to Fairhope, I called my mama to tell her that I was coming home and that Rush didn't want to come back with us. Mama never did like him since I ran off to Montana, so she didn't care enough to ask for any details. "I always told you he was no good," she said. I imagine she was waiting nine long years to say that.

She was more excited to show me her new bathroom floor the moment I stepped foot in Oklahoma than she was concerned about where Rush Kilmer might be, or why he let his girlfriend and daughter walk out of his life.

"Come see the floors that I got down at the grocery store!" she yelled from the door when she heard my taxi on the gravel drive. She was beaming as we stood inside the small bathroom. "It's that fancy vinyl plank. I ripped out all the linoleum and laid it myself. I just had to take one of those box cutters to trim it up. Have you ever seen anything like it?"

I had seen something like it. Too many times, to be exact. The faux oak grain looked more familiar than I wanted it to. Rush and I had the exact same planks in the kitchen and bathroom of the house that we rented. It had looked so pretty and fancy in our apartment, but as I stood with my mama in the bathroom, it just reminded me of Rush and what I'd done.

That night, and for most nights thereafter, I had to pretend I was in Montana again. It was the only way I could sleep.

The days weren't any easier. I didn't have no way to fill my time besides taking care of Penny, so I spent them online. People went crazy over Rush's disappearance, and armchair detectives would get together in discussion forums and post their theories about what happened to him. Some of those theories were about me and what I might've done to Rush. Those were the ones that I hated the most.

I'd spend all day reading those posts. Once I started, I couldn't stop.

My mama found me sitting on the couch one day with my phone in my hand. It was a few months after we moved back, sometime in the fall of 2013. Penny was sitting on the floor, real close to the TV so that she could kiss the screen whenever her favorite character came on.

"Honey, what's wrong?" Mama asked when she saw the look on my face. She put her arm around me, and I leaned into her soft shoulder.

Where was I s'pposed to start? I was a thirty-year-old single mom, broke and living with my parents. My mama sure couldn't help me out with money, what with my pa's drinking and all, and I felt stuck, more stuck than if I had stayed in that horrible Silverheel. And then there were, of course, the online posts. I handed her my phone to show her a string that I read so many times, I could recite it by heart:

TinTinTown - May 3, 2013 at 9:05 AM - wrote:

Those mountains are tough to survive in. I've hiked them a few times myself. If he went out there and didn't know what he was doing, it's entirely possible that he just got turned around and died from hypothermia or starvation. It happens all the time to inexperienced hikers. What I don't understand, though, is why the girlfriend didn't go looking for him. She drove back to Oklahoma almost immediately after reporting him missing.

RJ7890 - May 4, 2013 at 12:31 PM - wrote:

Yeah, but I read that he went winter camping all the time. I doubt someone with that much experience wouldn't be able to survive up in the mountains, even if they did run into trouble.

Badwater562 - May 4, 2013 at 12:55 PM - wrote:

Rush pissed off the wrong person. I've lived in Silverheel before. If you make enemies, you're on your own. The police don't care.

EKilmer - May 4, 2013 - wrote:

Yeah, like his girlfriend. There's no way that the girlfriend wasn't involved in this. I think he wanted out of the relationship, and she didn't want to lose custody so she poisoned him and buried his body in the mountains. There's no way he would've just ran off and left his baby daughter.

"I just can't believe I was so stupid," I said.

It's in the past, let it go, is what Rush would've told me if he was there, which is ironic given what I now know about him. But that was just another way that I was nothing like Rush. The regret ate at me. I had to find a way to rationalize all the stupid mistakes that I made—to make all of it worth it.

Mama looked at me like she didn't know how to say the words that were about to come out of her mouth. "Darling, Eli just called. They believe Rush is dead. He's been missing for so long; they fig're he must be gone. It's in God's hands now."

She rubbed my back, expecting me to be upset. I s'ppose my face probably did look upset, but it wasn't because of the news. I should've been happier that they wouldn't be looking for Rush no more. That was good news. I just had a hard time being happy those days.

Mama mistook my reaction for grief over Rush's s'pposed death, and she came up with something that she thought would get my mind off things.

"Why don't you walk down to the market and get us some stuff for supper," she said as she handed me a debit card.

I did as she asked, but I was kicking myself for taking Penny once we got to the market. She was only sixteen months or so, but she kept pointing at every brightly-colored toy and treat that she saw. I wasn't sure how much money was on the debit card, and I didn't want to risk it, so I had to keep telling her no. But each time she pointed, my heart broke a little more.

When we got to the register, she spotted a chocolate bar, her fav'rite. I caved and handed it to her, all the while holding my breath as I swiped the debit card.

Declined! the loud, beeping card machine seemed to scream.

I dug through the grocery bags and picked out the ground beef. I handed it to the cashier with a look that I hoped would say, "Please put this back for me. We can have meatless spaghetti, but I can't take the chocolate from my daughter."

The cashier must've understood because she looked embarrassed for me. Fortunately, though, Penny was absolutely clueless.

As we walked towards the exit, minus the ground beef, a shiny coin caught Penny's eye. It was partway under a shelf—hidden so well that it was something that only a sixteen-month-old would've spotted. She bent down to pick it up off the floor.

"You know who this is from?" I asked her. "Your Pa. He always used to say that he'd drop us a dime when he wanted to say hi."

Rush somehow willed the dime there; I just knew it. I just wasn't sure if Rush left the dime to say hello or to tell me he was going to rat me out.

There was a lady standing near where Penny found the dime. She was looking through a rack of paperbacks. In her hand was a book with a gold sticker that read, "Best seller! Over fifteen million copies sold!"

"Excuse me, ma'am. Is this yours?" I asked her as I held out the dime.

"No, dear. Thanks, though." She gave me a double take. "Hey, aren't you—"

No good deed goes unpunished. I knew where this was going. After Rush disappeared, I could barely go outside. Everyone always wanted to know what it was like to live with Rush. To have someone you love go missing.

I nodded my head and stood there politely as she rattled off the same questions as the rest of them:

"Tell me about him" was always the first question.

I never knew what to say to that one because Rush never really told me anything about himself. Not anything that was true, anyways.

"He, um, well, he was really adventurous," I replied, hoping that would be enough of a description.

"Wow, I can't imagine how sad you must be."

"Yeah, I miss him," I'd tell people, even if that wasn't necessarily true. I'd look like a monster otherwise.

"You know, you should write a book about his disappearance," the lady said as she pointed to the rack of books with the gold stickers. "I bet it'd sell as good as any of these."

"How much do you think those authors get for each book?" I asked her.

The lady weighed the book in her hand as if authors were paid by the pound. "Oh, I'd imagine a dollar or so for these tiny paperbacks."

I had a lot of confidence going in. I went straight home and sat in front of my computer. My fingers hovered over the keyboard, ready to start typing something, anything, but nothing came. Was it possible to have writer's block before you even started writing? My doubt grew each time the cursor blinked on the blank, white page. *Why did I think that I could do this? I've never written anything in my life.* Although, equally as true was the fact that I never failed at anything in my life. So, I told myself that this was going to be no different. It was just a novel. Thousands and thousands of words strung together to tell a story in a way that is interesting to the reader with no plot holes or inconsistencies. That's it. No big deal.

I wish that I could say that I was one of those prolific authors who can just sit down and write for hours on end, forgetting to eat or even sleep, and whose ideas come faster than they can hit the keys. But for the rest of 2013 and most of 2014, I sat in front of that computer screen, until, finally, some semblance of a book appeared.

When I was done, I sealed it in an envelope and mailed it to my literary agent, Joan.

"Gen, it's wonderful!" she exclaimed over the phone. "We just need a bio. Get it to me stat."

Stat. I think that was Joan's favorite word. *We need your revisions stat, Gen. I need you to sign off on these changes stat, Gen.* My shoulders fell. I thought I was done writing. But after the same, slow writing process, I finally had a bio:

> *The author grew up in Fairhope, Oklahoma. She has a daughter and has learned to live and write by one core belief: People are always so much better in theory.*

About two years from the day I typed my last

word, my book arrived in the mail. I turned the smooth cover in my hands and flipped through the pages. It was my own story about Rush—another version of what happened that icy February in Silverheel, Montana. I couldn't very well use his real name (or mine), so I called him Rush, since he was always running. And I called me Imogen Delilah Mae because I always did like those names.

It was a book about a guy who doesn't realize what happens when you trap an animal, and a girl who was left with no choice but to fight for her life. The guy disappears, like so many bodies do—to accidents, suicide, running away, and outright murder. His family, along with the rest of the world, is left wondering what happened to him.

At least, that's how my story went anyways. Most of it was a lie, of course—a story more unbelievable and outlandish than all the other theories that those amateur detectives could come up with on the internet. The truth is that no one will ever find out what happened to Rush Kilmer in February of 2013 at the top of that mountain in Montana. That's a secret that I'll take to my grave.

Those internet sleuths can throw around theories and try to fig're out what happened to people until they're blue in the face, but the truth is that only The Missing know. The Missing and me.

ABOUT THE AUTHOR

L. C. Rung

LC grew up in middle America, and much of her work is influenced by life in the midwest. She dreampt of being a novelist since middle school, where she typed stories on the school computer during her "study hall" period.

She took a brief detour and taught college after earning her PhD in communication from Ohio University. Since then, she has returned to her favorite pasttime: writing.

BOOKS BY THIS AUTHOR

Horse: A Novella

Hannah and JR live with their ten-year-old son, Arlo, in a tiny house on the lake. Their relationship is dysfunctional, complicated by drugs, depression, and an affair. Arlo is a meek little boy, living in the shadows of their relationship and receiving little in the way of acknowledgement.

Things likely would have continued this way, but a chance meeting with a new friend changes everything. Arlo's new friend gives him hope for a brighter future, one where he can be free of his parents' indifference. No one ever expected the innocent friendship to lead detectives to two dead bodies at the lake house. Who is responsible for their deaths? And where is Arlo?

Made in the USA
Monee, IL
27 July 2021